the *mind*

the reluctant romantics
book two

KATE STEWART

The Mind
The Reluctant Romantics (Book 2)
Copyright © 2016 Kate Stewart

Second edition edit by Donna Cooksley Sanderson
Cover Design: *QDesign*
Formatting: *Champagne Book Design*

dedication

For those who still believe in love at first sight.

The Mind Spotify playlist
https://spotify.link/gxyKEcgPaDb

prologue

Grant

"Momma?" I called out as I ran up the steps to our front door, already out of breath from the walk from the bus stop where she usually met me. Today she wasn't there waving at me from below the window when the bus pulled up. This morning, she told me she wasn't feeling good. Since Christmas, she's been in bed a lot. I know she doesn't want me to hear her cry, so she keeps the door shut, but I've been leaving my favorite Tonka trucks by her door so she knows I want to make her feel better.

"I'll be staying with my sister in Abilene," I heard my momma say. My daddy started to yell, and cold chills from the sweat drying made me shiver in the heat. I hated when Daddy yelled. He did it all the time now. Momma got sad, and Daddy just yelled at her, making her more sick. I hated Daddy for it. Momma doesn't smile anymore, and I know daddies are supposed to make mommas smile. My best friend Garrett's daddy made his momma smile all the time. My daddy just yelled at her when she talked.

"You aren't going anywhere with my son!" I heard him boom.

"Keep your voice down. He'll be home any minute, and I want us to explain this to him together."

"Explain what? That you've lost your marbles, and you're abandoning him?"

"I'm leaving you, Davis. You. Let me make that clear—"

I couldn't think beyond hearing her say she was leaving. Opening the door, I ran inside, finding them in the bedroom. Momma was packing as Daddy blocked the door. I pushed past him and ran to my momma, who was stuffing shirts into her full suitcase.

"Momma, why? Why are you leaving?" Momma looked at me in surprise, then started to cry.

"I'm going to stay with Aunt Jackie for a while."

My chest started to ache as I looked at my daddy head-on. "Is it because he yells at you all the time when you're sad?" He took a step back as if I'd kicked him, and I felt good about it.

"No, Grant, this isn't Daddy's fault," she said, taking my hand as she sat on the bed before pulling me to her.

"I need you to be a big boy now. You're almost seven years old, and look at you…walking from the bus stop all on your own."

"Yeah, I wasn't even scared," I said, puffing out my chest a bit. She smiled, but it wasn't the one I wanted her to give me. It wasn't the best one she had.

"Can you do that for me every day? Can you be a big boy and do your homework and chores while I'm gone?"

"Momma, don't leave." I turned to Daddy, who just stood there and watched Momma as she started to pack again. "Daddy won't yell no more. Will you, Daddy? Tell her!"

My daddy stayed silent. I knew I wasn't supposed to cry, but my stomach hurt too much. I looked at my daddy through narrowed eyes. "Daddy, tell her you'll listen to her like she asks you to all the time. Tell her you won't yell at her anymore!"

A small sob escaped my momma's lips as she shut the suitcase. "Grant," she whispered, "don't blame this on your daddy."

"It's his fault, Momma. Don't go. I'll listen to you. I'll take care of you when you're sick." She bent down to give me a kiss as she held me to her so tightly, I couldn't breathe. I pushed away from her to look at my daddy again.

"Don't you let her leave!" I didn't recognize my voice as I said, *"I'll hate you, Daddy. I'll hate you. This is all your fault."* I gripped the handle of my momma's suitcase and tried to pry it away from her.

"Grant, I'll be back in a couple of weeks. Let go...Grant... Davis!" Momma looked at Daddy to help her, and he took a step toward me. As soon as he reached me, I started to fight him. My momma's skirt brushed past the bedroom door, and the pain in my stomach got worse.

"Don't, Momma! Don't go!" I fought my daddy's grip as hard as I could. He audibly exhaled, and I looked up to see a teardrop rolling down his cheek. I was happy to see it. I was glad he was hurting, too.

"I'm so sorry, son."

"No, you aren't. You made her leave! I heard you tell her you couldn't help her. That you were tired of trying to help her!" I managed to get one arm free and then the other, but I already knew it was too late. I hated him more than ever as I chased her blue pickup down the drive.

I couldn't catch her, so I picked up rocks from the gravel path and threw them as hard as I could. One hit the tailgate, but the truck kept moving. I threw rock after rock as I cried so hard my sight became blurry, screaming promise after promise to her.

"Come on, son, come inside."

Ignoring him, I kept throwing rocks until I was so tired, I couldn't lift my arms. Even more tired than when I played all day in the woods with Garrett. Wiping my tears away with a dirty hand, I turned around to face my daddy.

"If you loved her like a daddy 'posed to, she wouldn't be gone!"

He nodded before turning around to walk back into the house. The screen door slammed behind him, and I jumped at the sound. I'd never talked to my daddy like that. Usually, he'd spank me real good, then talk to me about respect. I wondered if he would have the strap on the bed when I got inside. I didn't care. It was his fault Momma left, and he knew it. I wouldn't even cry if he strapped me.

I'd show him.

I walked back up the stairs and towards my bedroom, ready to face my punishment, but he never came.

I blinked hard against the recollection of that day as I pulled into campus, sighing at the usual traffic I had to fight to get there. I'd spent the hours on the road from Tennessee thinking about the shitty task ahead of me and about the day my mom left my dad and how horrible it felt. He'd brought another woman home a little over six months after she left, but it didn't last long. He's been alone ever since. My momma was alone, too, right up until she died a year ago. My whole life, I knew they still loved each other, but they were too stubborn to do a damn thing about it. Maybe they weren't meant to be, but there's something to be said about never picking up the pieces of your life and moving on with someone else twenty-two years after your divorce. I could only speculate what they did to ease the ache when I was between their homes in Texas and Tennessee, but to my knowledge, neither one ever fell in love again. Now, my mom was gone, and my dad was close behind.

I pressed my forehead to the steering wheel, stuck in a line of cars waiting to park, dreading the words I was about to say. I'd wasted another six months in a dead-end relationship, and now I had to be the one to break it off. Maybe it was the lingering guilt of remembering my mom leaving and the look on my dad's face—which I knew now was devastation—which was making this feel harder than it should be.

However, *this* was nothing like *that*. This wasn't love at all. This...was strangely pathetic, a new low for me. She wasn't even my type, yet I'd led her on a little bit by just staying in the relationship—if you could even call it that. No, if this feeling were anything like the way I felt when my momma left, I wouldn't be here ready to break it off. I would be holding on for dear life, making every effort to ensure we stayed together and that she was happy. I was no fool, and if the day ever came that I felt that way—*that* fear, *that* type of panic over losing a woman—I would do everything in my power to keep her, whoever she may be.

A horn sounded from behind me, and I lifted my gaze from the steering wheel with tired eyes. Hours of driving and fatigue seeped through my bones. All I wanted to do was sleep. This could wait.

A text came through just as a spot opened.

You coming? I'm so nervous! Please!

Fuck.

"Might as well get this over with," I muttered to myself. I put the truck in park and observed the students scattering to get to class. Still reluctant to drag my ass inside, I watched a few of them screw with their cell phones as they completely ignored the world around them. Rolling my eyes at their stupidity, I rolled down my window and killed the ignition, letting the hot breeze blow through the cab. It didn't make sense to me to ignore the world for a bunch of technology. I understood its purpose and used it myself, but spending day in and day out with their heads buried in other people's lives while life went on around them made these scholars look like idiots. I had no desire to drown myself in other people's lives when I fought night and day for a life of my own. My private time was precious. Between watching my dad wither away, caring for him, and ensuring I kept a job I loved, I reveled in the hours I could call my own. I'd be damned if I spent them wondering what everyone else was up to—every second mattered. Every. Fucking. Second. Including the seconds I was wasting in the cab of my truck, delaying the inevitable.

I could make some excuse and go nod off for a few hours.

As I straightened in my seat to do just that, I looked to the right of me as light broke through the heavy clouds, and a blinding ray of Texas sunlight lit up the campus grounds. As my eyes adjusted to the intrusion, I noticed a fair-skinned redhead sitting under a tree, deep in thought.

It was an awareness I'd only felt once in my life, and I recalled it all too well: Sharon Dunn, freshman year, a perfect little blonde-haired, doe-eyed beauty. I knew the first time I saw her, I had to make her mine. Even after she ripped my heart out and fell in love with my best friend, Garrett, I knew there would always be something special about her, even if she belonged to someone else. No, this awareness was like a brick to the head.

Scrutinizing her through the windshield, I watched her scratch her leg with her bare foot as she bit her lip in concentration while scribbling in a small notebook. Suddenly, every single piece of me was awake and hyper-focused on the woman who was now gathering her books. I remained motionless as I watched her stand then slide on her shoes. She was absolutely perfect from root to tip, and I couldn't help but lean forward to drink her in. More and more awareness crept over me as I watched her battle the wind for a few scattered pieces of paper that had fallen out of her binder. Giving up on the last piece and letting it fly through the air freely, she finally composed herself and began walking towards the same building I was supposed to be headed toward. As if graced by some gift, she paused in front of my truck, pulling something out of her bag and fastening it around her wrist. She looked my way briefly but didn't see me watching her before she hurried again in the direction of the other students. I strained to watch her go, realizing my hand was already on the handle when that last piece of paper she'd missed flew up and folded around the antenna of my truck. Watching the forgotten paper flapping in the wind like a neon sign, I paused briefly before I jumped out, chest on fire as I snatched it like the precious breadcrumb it was. I read the simple words scribbled all over it, and smiled before I tucked it into my pocket. I followed closely behind her as everything in me repeated in overdrive: *Go get her.*

chapter
one

Rose

I HELD MY BAG CLOSE TO MY CHEST AS I WALKED INTO THE crowded, stadium-style classroom filled with one hundred and sixty-plus students. Running my hands through my hair, I attempted to tame my mess of curls into something acceptable. Taking the first seat available, I quickly decided to give up on my hair and used the tie around my wrist to secure it into a bundle on top of my head. I had patiently waited for Dr. McGuire's class for three and a half years, and today was orientation. He would be prepping us throughout the lecture, but only a select few of us would be under his watchful eye during clinical rotations. I opened my bag to grab a pen, and it was immediately shoved away by the person sitting next to me.

"That seat's taken."

"Really?" I snapped sarcastically, fire burning in my cheeks.

"Yeah, really." The girl confronting me had a gorgeous face with large blue eyes and devastatingly beautiful, long brown hair—as if that wasn't a bigger kick in the teeth. She was rude and beautiful, and I found it disgusting.

"I'll move." I had no time for petty shit, and I refused to let the bad vibes of one rude girl ruin my day. I stood, then turned to enter the stairway leading to the next row and smacked right into who I supposed she was waiting for. I apologized, backed away then my gaze landed on his mouth. A full–lipped, broad grin led up to dark blue eyes that stole the air from my lungs. I had no choice but to smile back, but not before making a snide comment about his companion.

"She's *all* yours."

I pushed past him to take a seat on the other side of the stairs. When I looked back, he was still grinning at me as he took his seat. I made sure to memorize what I could because I wasn't looking back again. His dark, silky jet-black hair seemed to be all one length, and it flowed freely around his ears.

More perfect hair.

I hated my wavy red hair. It wasn't the bright Opie-red display that some other poor redheads had to sport, freckles and all—thankfully, I had none. However, true to ginger style, my skin was a pale white, and my eyes were the same jade green as my dad's. I had my mom's features: full lips, a strong nose, and a heart-shaped face. As far as redheads went, I got the best of it, though I still hated my hair. Mr. and Mrs. Perfect Hair irritated me immediately, but I quickly dismissed them both when the professor appeared.

Dr. McGuire exuded the hell-on-earth demeanor I'd heard about over the years. He wasted no time telling us we were useless, had no chance, and all hope would be lost by the time the semester ended. I found it laughable that he deemed it appropriate considering most of us only had a semester remaining before we graduated. Some of the students were already knee-deep in their specialty and had semi-smooth sailing from here on out—aside from passing the fourth-year boards. The other med students lucky enough to be under clinical rotation with Dr. McGuire for the rest of the semester had chosen the hard road, but it came with a perk. He was one of the best general surgeons in the country. I was going to ace this round. He offered only one spot per year to a promising surgeon for residency. If chosen, the new doctor was put through a rigorous interview. If they didn't make the cut, he would wait for a group of fresh students. It was a one-shot deal, and I intended to take mine. It wasn't even a question. I smiled at the good doctor as if to say, "bring it." By the time he had tried his best to discourage the class, I couldn't help but grin smugly at the intimidated faces around me that were twisted in pain. It wasn't that I was overly confident—it was that I knew I was close to doing what I was born to do.

Careful, Rose, remember what Mom says about karma kicking your ass.

And what Dad says: "There's nothing wrong with being a little smug. Confidence is vital."

I had no idea how they had managed to raise me without some sort of personality disorder or complex. My parents were so different, yet still madly in love. When I started school, I'd decided that love could wait. Well, after my one and only boyfriend threw me away for someone that looked more like the girl I'd taken a seat next to. I envied girls like that, so well put together at all times—the right clothes, the right shoes, perfect hair and skin tone, no matter the weather. I, however, was a hot mess and had been since I was a kid. Growing up, I had absolutely no interest in playing Barbies with my sister when I could be swinging from trees. When we were younger, Dallas used to come in from playing to show our parents she hadn't gotten her clothes dirty, while I, to my mom's absolute horror, brought in anything that crawled or hopped. As I watched the girl next to me play with her perfectly painted nails, I swore to myself that one day I would make time for things like that. I would become a better, more alluring version of myself.

Yeah, right.

School came first, love would have to wait, and my dad agreed wholeheartedly. On the other hand, my mom told me, *"The whole world would not make a damn bit of sense until I fell in love."* I'd already tried that and had barely made it out alive. My parents were a pair of romantics. While I did subscribe to their brand of thought, right now was not the time.

Curiosity got the best of me, and I turned to my left, although I had sworn to myself I wouldn't, and felt the prick of a tingle start from my scalp then down my back as I found his eyes on me. Turning my attention back to the lecture, I cursed my stupid curiosity. Why was he still looking at me?

When we were dismissed, I stood up to make my way to my apartment to read what I could to prep for my next lab. But I was stopped short at the door by the same man who had already taken up too much of my imagination. I pushed past him for the second time but was stopped in the corridor when he addressed me.

"You." It was a statement from him, not a question.

I turned to look at him, utterly confused. "Me?"

I noticed his girlfriend eyeing our exchange as she continued to talk to her friends.

"What's your name?"

"Rose."

"Rose," he mimicked, his eyes still intent on mine. He stood with his hands in the pockets of his jeans as he continued to stare. I finally broke our gaze. He smiled at the ground momentarily, then looked at me again. "Okay." His smile was breathtaking. It was boyishly handsome on a face that screamed all man. I was supposed to be doing something. What was I doing? He had my full attention. I couldn't tear my eyes away. He was quite a bit taller than I was and had a broad chest that was torturing his pale blue T-shirt. He didn't belong in my class. He didn't belong in this school, and it was too easy to tell. He had a deep tan and looked to be a bit of a roughneck. We stared at each other for a full minute as I tried desperately to take all of him in, but he had too much body for me to compartmentalize. Between the bulges in his arms, his broad chest, and an ass I was straining to get a glimpse of, I concluded he looked like *Tarzan* in modern-day clothing. If I kept my appraisal of him going on any longer, I felt I would start spouting off things like: *"You Tarzan, me Jane, and me want to swing."*

"Okay, Rose," he said, interrupting my inner dialogue and daydream. Damn him! We were *almost* happy living in the trees. It was obvious he had something on his mind.

"Is there a conversation I'm having with you that I don't know about?" I asked in a hushed tone.

"Yes, Rose, there is." I was graced with another smile—*oh, God, a dimple*—then, "I'll see you around."

"Well...who are you?"

He looked back at me with a confidence that I'd only seen a few men carry—namely, my dad. "I'm the man that's going to marry you."

I snorted, quite unattractively, as my reply. Then he caught my gaze again, imploring me to believe him.

"I'm the man that *you* are going to marry." I couldn't stop myself. My jaw dropped. I didn't even know this crazy man's name, and we were getting married? The sincerity in his face, the look in his eyes, was serious.

"Okay...so what's your name, husband-to-be?"

"Grant." Hmph, I preferred *Tarzan.*

"Can't wait, Grant. When's the big day?"

He ran his hand through his beautiful hair, gave me one more thorough once over then winked before walking away. *Well, that wasn't weird. No, not at all.*

As I walked towards safety, I rubbed my upper arms, trying desperately to shake off the spell I'd just been put under. What a maniac. What a totally...lickable, delusional maniac.

Still slightly dazed from the oddest conversation I'd ever had, I felt my stomach growl and decided to forgo my apartment to join my roommate, Jennifer, at The Bistro. The Bistro was a local dive and a campus favorite. When I spotted Jen, I took a seat in the chair next to her. Her long copper hair was tied into a perfect, sleek ponytail, and her glasses rested on the tip of her nose. As far as bookworms went, I thought I was in competition for being the biggest...until I met Jen. She was my only close girlfriend at school. We'd hit it off right away on our first day of med school four years ago. She reminded me of my sister with her bold personality and confident demeanor. Although we didn't see eye to eye on most things, we had a fantastic friendship. She was more a fly-by-the-seat-of-her-pants-girl while I remained—to her—annoyingly disciplined. I would miss her terribly when we parted ways after graduation. She would be moving to California to marry her long-time beau, Alex, and I would stay in Texas, hopefully starting my residency with McGuire.

"I met the man that's going to marry me today. He told

me so," I said, interrupting her reading as I forked a bite of my salad.

"Really," she replied with amusement, her eyes not leaving the pages. "Is he hot?"

"Hotter than hell, and I've never seen him before today. There is no way he's a student."

"Trolling weirdo, huh?" she said, her nose still in her book.

"Must be. But I will tell you right now—he seemed serious. It was the first time in a long time that I wanted to do something extracurricular."

"Uh, Rose," Jennifer said, putting her book down to eye me.

"Sweet Jesus, he had long dark hair, but not greasy or gross, and not too long, either... Eww, I'd hate that. His eyes—dear God—and that mouth...I could spend hours on the anatomy of that mouth. His fucking arms—"

"Rose!" Jen, who was now laughing, gave me a nod.

"He's behind me, isn't he?"

"I'm not a piece of meat, you know." I heard him chuckle and felt my stomach revolt against me. I turned to find him smiling at me—again. I took in a long breath at the sight of him but swiftly recovered.

"Well, that's twice in one day, future husband. I'm honored. Can I help you?"

"Not yet." I felt my cheeks heat, but I was never one to shy away—especially from fun. I sensed the renewed electricity race through me from our earlier meeting until Ms. Perfect Hair approached us. I was instantly jealous. Why? I had no idea.

Well...he *was my* future husband.

I could tell my presence was beginning to annoy her when she eyed me with disdain, grabbed Grant's arm, and then walked away with him possessively. They were both un-hinged and deserved each other.

"Okay, if that was him, I don't care if he is batshit crazy. I would fornicate with him and have rabid babies." I watched Jen's reaction and felt justified in entertaining Grant for his looks alone.

"Told you," I said, resuming with my fork.

"Aren't you embarrassed?"

"Not really." I winced. "Jen, is that bad?"

"No, it's bold and awesome," Jen said before taking a sip of her drink, eyes still on Grant.

"I get it from my dad...well, and my mom. When it comes to what I want, dad, when it comes to speaking my mind, mom. I'm screwed, aren't I?"

"Probably," she answered, "but it's awesome."

"Lord, help me and my mouth through the rest of this year."

"He's not looking at you anymore. You must have scared him away."

"It was too soon for marriage." I felt a tiny tug in my chest but dismissed it.

Paging Dr. Rose Whitaker, please. I was instantly back where I started hours before.

chapter
two

Rose

A FEW DAYS LATER, I WAS ON MY CELL PHONE WITH MY SISTER as I sat under a tree on campus, the hospital in my direct line of sight. Dallas had just started her second year of residency at Dallas Memorial, a teaching hospital directly across the street from my campus, and where I made clinical rounds. On my first day of school, I'd sat under this same tree, studying the hospital for hours, dreaming of my future. Today I was attempting—in vain—to get a small amount of sun on my face and shoulders in my spaghetti strap, black sundress. The Texas sun bore down on me, the late August heat unforgiving.

I spent so much time in sterile, cold rooms and reveled in it. I had a book in my lap and was trying to get the rest of my bases covered over the weekend. I would not fail. This was my dream. It amazed our parents that both their little girls had the same one. It was never a competition between us. We had decided long ago to lift each other up. We helped each other through school with rigorous hours of studying together. I helped her prepare for tests and labs, and in turn, it helped me excel during my first few years. We were each other's biggest cheerleaders.

She and I were set on opening our own practice one day. We would offer a full-service practice with every specialty imaginable on-site. She would govern general medicine, and I would manage surgery. It was a shared dream, and we had worked for years to make it a reality. We were getting close—Dallas closer than I due to the additional training I'd need to become a surgeon. We both had a handful of years left, but it seemed like nothing compared to the long road we had traveled to get as far as we'd come.

"What's it like?" I asked, gripping my cell tight to my ear so I could hear every word, even though I knew the question would annoy her.

"I've already told you this a million times. It's exactly what you think—a lot like the rounds you make every day. It's nothing like the movies or TV shows. It's relatively boring until it's not, then wham! Intellectual orgasm.

"So, are you getting any?"

"Dallas, I swear you talk like a man," I huffed at her invasion.

"Good, sometimes I wish I was a man. Use this time wisely. Next thing you know, you will be held down by the same penis over and over."

I quickly baited her. "Stop acting like you hate Josh. You love him."

"Sure I do." I could hear the sarcasm drip over the line. "I'm being paged. I love you, Rosie."

"You know I hate that!" I snapped at her nickname for me. Suddenly the book disappeared from my lap, and I gasped as Grant's face took its place.

"What is it? What's wrong?" Dallas asked in a panic.

"Uh...nothing, Dallas. I just spilled...something in my lap." His smile was mischievous, and I felt a strange urge to...kiss him. He placed my hand on the top of his head, and I began stroking his hair without hesitation. It was pure dark silk. What in the *hell* was I doing playing along? I had to get this man away from me. Surely the psychiatric hospital missed him.

"Dallas, weren't they paging you?" I asked, losing all train of thought as Grant's blue eyes pierced me from below.

"Yeah," she replied, clueless about the man-God staring up at me. "I fell asleep up against the wall."

I let out another laugh at Dallas and Grant, who was pantomiming a conversation with his hands.

"Love you, Big D," I said with a smile, retaliating against her usage of my nickname by throwing hers back at her.

"Bitch."

"Talk to you soon." I hung up and pushed the intruder's head off my lap. He chuckled as he took a seat in front of me, our knees touching.

"I've been looking all over for you. I wanted to see you before I left."

"Still listening to the voices in your head, huh?" I said, placing my book so it rested on my stomach and chest as if it could protect me.

"I know I must seem a little crazy to you, but I'm running out of time." He leaned in closer, and I felt goosebumps form. His massive arms and chest were ripped to perfection under his collared T-shirt. He was close and even more devastating than I'd initially thought. "I know what needs to happen. I just can't do anything about it now," he offered as if he was apologizing.

"And I suppose I have no say in this whatsoever? I've heard

a story like this before." I was referring to my parents' rocky fifteen-year start. "I can tell you it's a bad idea. Besides, you have a girlfriend."

"No, I don't."

"From what I saw, you have a very possessive girlfriend. You know the brutal bitch brunette—"

"I live too far away," he murmured as he inched closer, ignoring my protest.

My voice got louder as I got nervous. "Well, there you have it. The epic story of Rose and Grant, a tragic two-minute affair!"

He took my face in his hands and leaned in, his eyes burning a hole through me. I was shaking and couldn't keep my lower lip still. He noticed and brushed his thumb over it, attempting to soothe me.

Holy shit!

"I knew you would come around." He grinned as he closed the remaining distance between us. I couldn't stop it. It was a simultaneous failure of limbs and brain cells. His lips touched mine softly, and I let out an unexpected moan. He pulled back and watched me, hands still on both sides of my face. "Did you feel that?"

I nodded my head in agreement as he slowly leaned in again. He touched my lips with his, and I felt everything I possessed start to tingle. His tongue gently delved into the corners of my mouth, and I opened it, inviting him in, letting him take the rest of me. I knew it was insane, as insane as the hot man sticking his tongue into my mouth, but I didn't care. What could it hurt? My defenses crumbled, and I let Grant have his way with me. My hands instinctively wrapped around his massive biceps as he plunged his tongue in sweetly until there was nothing left to taste. When he pulled away, our foreheads touched briefly before his eyes again penetrated mine.

"Rose, God, it was better than I thought it would be. I knew it would be...like this."

"Look, Grant—"

"Don't," he said. "You know you felt it, too."

"And it felt good. Just don't do it again, okay? Your *girlfriend* is walking over here and is about to kick my ass!"

He spun to see her rapidly approaching as she shrieked, "You break up with me, don't leave campus, and two days later, you're kissing someone else!"

He turned to me, amusement on his face. "Well, I have to go. I *will* see you again. And you were right about her." He smiled, pecked my lips, and then stood to shield me from her wrath. She was beyond hostile. I wasn't looking forward to that eventual confrontation.

After a hasty goodbye, I spent the remainder of the afternoon sitting under the tree with a book in my lap, but I couldn't read one word. Not one single word.

～

One Week Later

"Wake up, beautiful."

A warm hand lay on my cheek, but I felt too soothed to find the energy to open my eyes. I leaned into the reassuring weight, enjoying the comfort of my dream.

"Wake up, sleeping beauty. We don't have much time."

I sat straight up in my bed, gasping in shock at the man

hovering over me. I recognized him, but it did little to calm the panic racing through me.

"Grant? What in the hell are you doing in my bedroom?!"

"I'm sorry. I didn't mean to scare you." He smelled incredible like he was freshly showered. I ignored it in lieu of the terror of having a stranger in my bedroom.

"What about this isn't creepy, Grant?"

"Your roommate let me in."

"Jennifer!" I loved her dearly, and I would miss her.

Grant gave me a rueful smile that showcased his perfect dimple. "She left."

"Oh, I *am* going to kill her!" I started to get out of bed, but he stilled me before speaking gently as if I were a caged animal.

"Don't be upset. I assured her you were in good hands."

I blinked repeatedly to clear the lingering sleepiness and studied him carefully. His expression was amused but heated. His dark hair flowed around his face, and his bulging arms rested on my knees as I pulled my comforter closer. Grant pulled his full lips into his mouth as if he wasn't exactly sure what he was doing in my room either.

"Seriously, Grant, get out of my room and apartment."

He seemed to make up his mind on something before he spoke. "I came to see you. I know it's late. I was hoping to spend a little time with you."

I looked at the clock and saw it was 11 P.M.

"I'm a fourth-year med student, Grant, and I need my sleep. I threw the comforter off me, saw him glance at my black negligee, and was suddenly thankful that I had chosen it to wear tonight of all nights. Usually, it was a stained T-shirt and boy shorts, or worse. His eyes immediately found mine, and I sucked in a deep breath.

"I don't know how they do things where you're from, but this is not the norm here!" I was reacting the way I should, but I really wasn't afraid. Although I had labeled him crazy, I didn't believe it to be true. Delusional, maybe, but not completely crazy.

"Look, Rose, I know I'm being a creep, but if you don't get some clothes on right now, I will kiss every inch of skin I see."

"The hell you will," I said, praying for just one second that he would make good on his threat.

He leaned in close before he whispered, "Where should I start?"

"I'm up. Now turn around."

Sighing heavily, I grabbed the jeans off the floor and slipped them on. I raced to my closet and grabbed a sweatshirt and bra before making my way to the bathroom.

What in the *hell* was he doing here? Was Jennifer out of her mind? Did she care so little for me that she trusted me in the hands of a stranger? And who in the hell comes to visit a woman this late? I quickly changed, brushed my teeth, and met him in my living room. He was scanning the photos on our wall but then stopped, standing directly in front of one of me. When he noticed me in the room, he turned and gave me a smile that nearly knocked me on my ass. I couldn't help but smile back and was sure my next statement held no weight because of my stupid grin.

"This is not okay. You have to go, and I've got two labs tomorrow."

"Just give me an hour or two, okay? I really want this time with you."

"Why? You don't know me...like at all."

"I know a few things. I know you were a total nerd in

college and dated the same guy all four years. I know that you eat like a man and you love rap music. I also know you haven't been on a date in a year."

"What?! How do you know all that?" I crossed my arms in front of my chest, both embarrassed and defensive.

"I've been to The Bistro every day this week looking for you. I found Jennifer. She's easy to bribe. Let's go."

"And my address?" I ask suspiciously.

"Same scenario," he said dismissively as if it weren't important.

"Where could you possibly take me this late?"

He was like a tree in my living room, a walking, talking, beautiful tree, solid and strong, as he replied, "It's a surprise."

"A 'drag me into the woods where no one finds my body for months, and I deteriorate in the hot Texas sun, being eaten by wild animals' surprise'?"

"Look, I know it's less than the ideal time for a date, but I just got off my shift and don't have much time left. Will you just please take my word for it? This isn't how I normally do things, and, Rose, I could never hurt you. You could only hurt me." I looked at his face and saw his sincerity, but I still wasn't biting.

"Give me your license," I demanded.

"What?"

"You heard me," I said, holding out my hand. "If I'm going to leave my apartment with a complete stranger, I'm going to need some insurance."

He reached into his back pocket and chuckled as he handed me his license. I walked over to my computer desk, scanned it in, and attached it to an email to Dallas, stating that if I ended up missing, this was the man who took me.

He peered over my shoulder and let out a loud laugh. "She ought to enjoy that tomorrow."

Turning back to look at him, he winked and pulled his keys from his pocket. "Rose, I know this isn't the best way to try and date you, but trust me when I tell you, for me, it's the only way right now." I felt for him as he attempted to explain his insanity and decided to cut him a break.

"I really don't think you would hurt me, but just in case, they may have enough to prosecute."

"I thought you were studying to be a doctor?"

"Don't ever compare me to a lawyer, Grant," I said, grabbing my purse that conveniently held a small can of mace. Okay, maybe I wasn't one hundred percent sure he wouldn't hurt me. What I was certain of was that Jennifer was going to have hell to pay.

We piled into his gigantic Chevy truck and headed out on I-35. A few minutes into our ride, I began to question him.

"Really, Grant, what is all this about?" Everything in me told me 'fight or flight' was what I should be feeling, yet I was eerily at ease.

His answer was direct and simple as he kept his eyes on the road. "I just want to get to know you."

"Why?"

"Let's just say I've had a good feeling about you since the minute I saw you. 'Sides, I have a thing for redheads." I saw his smirk and turned in my seat to face him.

"I hate my hair."

"Now that's crazy," he said, taking his hand off the wheel to stroke a lock behind my shoulder and smooth it down. I had to resist the urge to shiver.

He turned onto a country road, and all I saw were trees

and the bright light of the moon. I mentally prepared myself for war. Who would have guessed I would die in the hands of the most beautiful guy I'd ever met. It's then I realize that my safety net might be useless. Dallas doesn't even check her emails—I can't even remember the last time she replied.

Do the throat punch, Rose. It's most effective. You can't possibly fight your way out of this unless you go lethal. Lethal, think ninja, think Hannibal Lecter!

"I have a mean left hook and ammo," I sputtered nervously.

Great job, Rose. You're dead.

"Rose, listen to me. I would never *ever* hurt you."

"Then why are we in scary territory?" I looked around, seeing nothing but trees, knowing we were alone for miles. Aside from our brief conversation, the silence in between was a little scary.

"This is my land, and it's my favorite place in the world. I want to be here with you," he said as the forest parted and we entered a small clearing.

I narrowed my eyes at him. "So, I know one thing about you. Were you born and raised here?"

"Yes, my dad lives in Tennessee. I've spent the last two years going back and forth. He's terminally ill, and I haven't been able to spend much time here this year. God, I miss it," he said, rolling down his window to let in the night air. I suddenly felt a little guilty for doubting him.

"I'm sorry, Grant. What's the diagnosis?"

"Cancer of the liver." He eyed me carefully before he set his jaw, struggling to mask what I was sure was pain. "He was a drunk for a short time, but I can't say he deserves this punishment now. It's a horrible thing to watch."

"I'm sure it is," I said sincerely. "Is there a specialist on his case?"

"No one will really give him the time of day at this point. Most just say it's hopeless and to make him comfortable. He can't really afford the health care he needs, and I think that's a huge reason why they won't treat him. I find doctors to be the worst people on earth." He smiled, and I scowled at him. "Present company excluded."

"That's bullshit. Someone will see him. I know a few doctors that—"

"I've tried everything," he said emphatically. He shook his head, warding off his evident pain. "Look, I really do want to tell you more, but not tonight, okay? I deal with that daily, and tonight I want to be a little selfish. I have done nothing but think about you since our kiss under the tree."

"I wish I could say the same." I laughed at his grim face. "Okay, I thought about it once...twice."

I got a flash of his dazzling white teeth and was happy I'd pleased him. He parked beside a small metal shack as I carefully surveyed the land. A small plastic white table sat under a large live oak with a huge fishing pond behind it. I could see the silhouette of ducks walking by. They would be the only witnesses to my pending murder.

"It's pretty damn dark out here," I noted, landing squarely from his monster truck to keep my balance.

"I've got this."

He pulled a large cooler out of the bed of his truck, followed by a smaller one then started unpacking it at the table under the tree. I laughed as he draped the table in white linen and lit a candle in the center. My nerves started to ease slightly as he took special care to set everything just right.

Don't get too comfortable yet, Whitaker. There is a thing called premeditation.

"I hope you brought your manly appetite." He placed an assortment of meats and cheeses on the table, along with shrimp cocktail and a ton of fruit.

"A picnic at night?"

"Why not?"

"You are certifiable."

He winked, then continued the task of setting up the table. "Name one date that you've been on that's been more romantic."

"Threatening to paw a girl while in her bed to get her to go out with you is *not* romantic." I took a look around and realized he was right. It was absolutely perfect outside. The full moon illuminated what his small candle didn't. Wasting no time, I devoured half of the cheese platter, then downed an ice-cold beer.

"You serve beer instead of wine. I love it," I complimented as I let out a throaty moan and devoured half of the shrimp. I didn't realize he was staring at me, mouth gaping until I was on my second beer.

"Jesus, Mary, and Joseph, woman, how the hell do you eat like that?" He lifted the table linen, looking underneath as if I hadn't just eaten my weight in food and was somehow hiding it.

I gave him a toothy grin. "I always have."

He turned the empty cooler upside down as if to poke at me some more. I smiled and started on the fruit. We made light conversation, and after a few minutes of silence on his part, I looked up to see him eyeing me.

"You...are beautiful."

I gave him a wary glance, looked down at my jeans and sweatshirt, then back up to meet his eyes.

"It doesn't matter." He sipped his beer and grabbed my hand. I let him hold it and felt the glide of his thumb as he stroked the top of it. Warmth spread through me, and I welcomed it. It had been so long since I felt a man's touch...way too long. I decided to entertain him, even if it was just for the night.

Tension began to ease out of my shoulders as we spent a few comfortable minutes in silence, listening to the wind breathe through the tree above us. It was slightly cooler now than it was when we'd first arrived.

It *was* heaven.

"Do you like it out here?" I shifted my attention away from the pond to capture his candlelit face. His eyes were smoldering, and I could feel the constant undercurrent between us. The source was an undeniable attraction. It excited me as much as it scared me.

"Yes, it's breathtaking," I answered, grabbing a fresh beer.

"Good, I'm going to build a house out here. I want you to like it."

"Grant, you can't really think we're getting married."

"Why not?" He shrugged his shoulders and sat back in his seat, sipping his beer before he continued. "Maybe it's not as common as it was back in yesteryear, but things like this—" he pointed between us, beer in hand "—do happen, and I'll prove it."

"How?"

"I've already started." He grinned, and with that grin, my pulse picked up. I entertained the idea of those full, curved lips covering my body.

"It's ridiculous. I hardly know you. In fact, I know nothing about you."

"I was born here, raised here, by my mom. She died a year ago. I was not a nerd like you. I played football. I dated...a lot...until recently. I'm twenty-nine. I work on airplanes as a mechanic, and I smoke weed. It's my only vice."

I spit out my beer, laughing harder than I had in months.

"So... you're a pothead?" I noted, my chuckle slowing.

"No, I smoke weed. It relaxes me," he defended weakly, but not in a way that made me believe he gave a damn what I thought about it.

"Same thing."

"No, it's not, actually," he said, matter of fact, as he packed the trash in his cooler.

"Whatever you say," I taunted, rolling my eyes.

I finished my third beer, grabbed another, and stood up to walk toward the ducks. Grant grabbed a blanket from the back of the truck, then met me at the edge of the pond. Once comfortable, I sat back, relaxed and willing to give this strange man more of a chance. I had been single far too long. And if I was even more honest with myself, it felt wonderful to have the attention of a good-looking man.

"I didn't realize I needed a break until you gave me one, so thank you."

"Rose, I want you to know I totally respect you and what you're doing. You know...in school. I'll try to make our dates a little bit easier on you. I did mean what I said about the doctors, though. I haven't had good luck with any of them, ever. It's always been bad news, but I'm hoping you change that."

"Who says I want to date you, Grant?" There was a playfulness in my voice, and I knew he heard it.

"You know you do."

"Wow...that's pretty presumptuous," I toyed.

"Maybe," he murmured. He seemed so confident at times, and others downright nervous. Maybe this wasn't the norm for him. He certainly didn't seem like the type that needed to kidnap a woman from their bed to take them on a picnic. His looks alone could land him any woman he wanted—of that, I was sure. Maybe he actually *did* want to know me. And maybe, just maybe, the night he had just presented me with had made me want to know him a little, too.

"I have to go back to Tennessee as soon as I leave you to take care of my dad. I also have to pick up a certain amount of hours to keep my job here. It's a crazy schedule, and the reason why I have to be a little resourceful with my time—but I will find the time. Will you, Rose?"

"Grant, you can't ask me for what I can't give." It was an honest answer. My schedule—though nothing like his—demanded everything I had. I was too close to the finish line.

"I will take that as a yes." I shrugged my shoulders and looked out at the pond. As insane as the night was, I felt at peace. Grant adjusted himself to sit behind me, then slid his arms around my waist—and I didn't resist. It had been way too long since I felt a man's touch. My career was my priority, but I refused to lose my entire life to it. I wanted to be a well-rounded surgeon—if those even existed. I had dreams beyond my career, and a family was definitely one of them. I credited my parent's marriage as the ringleader of that dream.

He pulled me close to him, my back to his chest. I leaned my head back and felt his breath on my neck. The goosebumps spread from my hairline to my toes, and I shivered at their arrival. His fingers caressed my neck, massaging lightly. I turned to look at his face and noticed a whisper of a smile on his lips. He leaned in to kiss me, but I took a sip of beer to block him. He laughed at my lame attempt to brush him off. If I let him touch me now, I was as good as gone. I was still a bit weirded out by the whole scenario, and yet everything in me was telling me to go for it, *at least* on the physical side. I was no man's plaything, but I had a healthy sexual appetite that I'd ignored for far too long.

"You know, Rose, I know you feel it, too. It's okay to be a little afraid. But this is how the good ones start."

"The good ones?"

"The great ones. This will be a great one." He pressed his lips in gentle kisses around the only exposed skin on my neck, then murmured, "And it will only get better when I finally get to touch you." I felt myself become damp at his words, and the trail he was blazing across my skin with the whisper of his lips set me on fire. There was no way I was getting out of this if it went any further. Sensing my hesitation, he quickly stood up.

"This is all I wanted. I can take you back now if you're tired."

"Thank you, Grant. This was beautiful, really. I won't forget it."

"Let's get you back in bed."

I stood up and watched him pack the truck as I folded the blanket and put it on top of the cooler. I looked at the clock and realized he had gotten a little more than his two hours. It seemed like just a few minutes. Time had flown with him.

We didn't speak at all on the way back. We simply took turns studying each other with brief glances as he drove. Pulling up to my apartment, my heart picked up its pace as I remembered our kiss beneath the tree on campus. He walked me to my door, and I turned to bid him goodnight, praying he would do it again.

"Oh no, Rose, I'm leaving you how I took you." Too tired to argue, I walked inside and climbed into bed.

"No... *just* how I left you."

"Really? The creep again?"

He ignored my comment. "I'm pretty sure it was a black negligee."

I raced to the bathroom, my stomach in knots. I had no idea what had gotten into this man, but I knew that his voice was close to sending me over the edge. It made no sense, but I went with it. I took a little longer than I should have in the bathroom, spritzing on some of Jen's high-dollar perfume that smelled incredible. I rubbed lotion on my legs, thankful that I'd shaved earlier. There was a man in my room that wanted me and who clearly needed prescription strength glasses. I was beginning to panic and decided to hell with it. If, for some reason, I had been granted a sprinkle of luck from the universe, I needed to take advantage.

"Jesus," he rasped out as he watched me walk across the room in my second skin. I couldn't help but shy away a bit and retreat under my comforter.

"No, don't cover up. Don't." Obeying the command of his sex-filled voice, I lowered it and let him take in all of me. He stood at the foot of my bed and watched me as my breathing took on a faster pace. He slowly took a seat next to me and reached out with his hand to caress my face. I was instantly hot. I felt my nipples harden as he traced his fingertips down my neck and outlined the hem of the fabric. I licked my lips in anticipation.

"Goodnight, Rose," he offered, pulling the covers over

me slowly and pushing off the bed to leave. "I can't kiss you goodnight. If I kiss you right now, I'm going to fucking lose it." I stopped him by gripping his hand, grabbing the back of his head without thinking, and bringing his mouth to mine. His lips brushed mine softly and then took my whole mouth, leaving me breathless. Our tongues tangled as he kissed me deeply, melting any common sense, any resolve I had been holding on to. I reached out, gliding my fingertips along the bulge of his arms and moaning into his mouth. I reached for his shirt, and he hesitated, pulling it down as I pushed it up over the hard ridges of his stomach.

He grinned down at me as he ripped himself away slightly to study me. "What's gotten into you, woman?"

"Opportunity," I whispered, slipping my tongue back into his mouth and hearing him groan. His body was rock hard beneath my fingertips, and I was dying to explore him more with greedy hands. Caution lights of any kind were swept underneath the bed he had me panting on. I was in need. He could fill that need. It was simple, except it wasn't. Grant's kiss was not only debilitating my reasoning but also made me insane with want. So, like any woman with a beautiful man between her legs, I began to argue with myself.

You hardly know him!
Yep.
He may very well be insane!
Uh huh.
You don't do one-night stands.
Nope.
What are you doing?!
Naked, get him naked.
This is not a good idea!

One more brush of the hard length with my hand and the whisper of his skilled tongue with mine, and the argument quickly changed.

It wouldn't hurt to have a look.

Just a peek.

You really have ranked below average in the penis count department.

I deserve this.

You so deserve this.

"I want you," I confessed. "Right now." His eyes, now molten, looked over my heated body as he helped me remove his shirt. As soon as he was bare-chested, I screamed an inward thank you to God and the universe. Another deep kiss and I was desperate to have him inside of me. He hovered over me, and I felt his sharp grunt as I gripped the thick bulge in his pants with my hand, making my intention clear.

"Rose," he pushed out through clenched teeth as I pulled his hand between my legs, "are you sure?"

I couldn't think of anything but the throbbing between my thighs. His fingers slipped beneath my panties, and he cursed a quick "fuck yes" before he pushed two fingers inside of me. "Grant," I panted as he pulled back from our endless kiss to watch my reaction to his hand.

"I want you, too...so fucking much, but are you sure?" I rocked into his hand as he rewarded me with even more pressure where I needed him most. I was seconds from coming as he leaned an inch above my face, watching my every move. With my mouth open and nothing but encouraging gasps coming out of me, he sucked my lower lip into his mouth as he stroked me with just the right amount of pressure. His fingers expertly slid up and down between my folds with so much skill that I exploded beneath him. Blinded by the feel of him, I let go as he coaxed the rest of my orgasm out of me, his head now buried in my chest, his breath heavy.

"Goddamn, woman, I'll never recover from that." I was too far gone to stop and had no intentions of doing so, anyway. This strange man had evoked a potent need in me that had laid dormant for too long. Although it was slightly sated from his touch, I had to have more.

I pushed him into a sitting position, lifting myself to my knees as I fidgeted with his jeans. When his rock-hard length broke free, I took it into my mouth, moaning in appreciation. I tasted the salt seeping from him and moaned again.

"Oh, fuck," he groaned as he caressed my back slowly with one hand while running his fingers through my hair with the other.

Once I had him close enough to the edge, I scrambled with the rest of his clothes, getting him naked, stroking him, sucking him until I could no longer control myself, and began begging him to release me from the ache that had once again built inside me. I grabbed a condom from my nightstand, placed it in his hand, and prayed it was still worth a damn—though I'd never missed a pill. Grant hesitated, still asking permission as I writhed beneath him.

"Grant, take it!"

"Yes, ma'am."

He stilled me and my restless hands and lips, searching my eyes. I found myself unable to meet his gaze and knew I was acting like a mad and desperate woman. He smirked as I shied away from him after such a blatant sexual display but didn't say a word as he stood and rolled on the condom. Never in my life had I been blessed to have such a man. My last serious boyfriend, David, had been built but had nothing on Grant. He stood proudly as he watched me pull off the scrap of silk that covered the rest of my virtue. I lay back in bed, taking him in, and he did the same. Muscle outlined every inch of him. His piercing, deep blue eyes held nothing but intense heat as I spread my legs for him in beckoning.

He gripped his thick length, pumping himself before me, making my mouth water. Eyes, lips, arms, abs, legs...him—all of him displayed out before me in teasing.

"Please...Grant, I know what I'm asking."

"I'm pretty sure you don't know what you're taking," he rasped out as he slowly moved to brace himself above me. His mouth descended, and I took in a breath as he kissed my stomach, then tongued his way across my breasts. "Sweet, so sweet," he murmured, rolling my nipple between his teeth.

"You," he heaved out, his breath a warm gust against my skin. I watched his chest rise and fall as he hovered over me, his beautiful dark hair falling around him. Now nestled between my thighs, he waited until I met his eyes before he pushed inside me. I cried out along with him, surprised at how amazing it felt. He went completely still, allowing me to get used to his size, his chest heaving faster, yet he hadn't moved. "You okay?"

"Yes. Please, keep going. I want you so much," I said, wrapping my legs around him, feeling him sink into me even further.

His lips came crashing down and stole my mouth in an all-out fit as our tongues thrashed together wildly. I felt myself start to sweat as he kissed me feverishly, leaving our bodies together but still not moving inside me. "Please, Grant."

"God, help me." He thrust himself again and hit me so deep I caught myself holding my breath as the orgasm crept up on me and then took over. He picked up his pace and began to drive into me, pounding out every bit of my pleasure and making it last. When it subsided, he rolled on his back and pulled me on top of him as he traced my throat with his tongue and gentle lips.

"Come again, Rose."

That was all I needed. I gave him what he asked for and cupped his sac, stroking him beneath us as I brought my hips up and down to meet his. "Grant, give it all to me."

He grabbed my hips, pushing them down on him, fusing us together, igniting me again as I matched his pace. I felt him growing close as he pulled me down hard onto him, wrapping his arms around me as we came together. I fell on top of his chest as we regained our senses, taking each other's breath in consolation before I fell on my back next to him.

We lay side-by-side, holding hands, not saying a word. I had no idea how he was feeling, but I was beside myself. What in the hell had I just done? And, *oh, God,* did I want to do it again. I would gladly give up medicine to feel that way every minute for the rest of my life. I heard him chuckle and turned to see him propped on his elbow.

"Cheese and beer, that was easy." I glared at him. "Kidding, baby, kidding! Oh...you're a feisty one."

"Shut up. I don't normally do that, Grant. Don't go assuming anything about me."

His dimple appeared as he gripped my chin in his free hand. "I'm assuming you take care of your men like you do your food—you devour them both."

I lifted my brow and gave him my best seductive smile. "Can't handle a little take charge in the bedroom, Grant?"

"On the contrary, baby. I've never been more pleasantly surprised."

"That's what happens when you sleep with strangers."

He made quick work of his lips, brushing them gently over my sweat-dampened skin as he reached for his jeans and pulled another condom out of his wallet.

"I'm going to need to repeat that, you know, just to make sure it was real," he whispered as he braced his arms above me, kissing my lips softly and in short repetition. "And Rose," he crooned as he pushed inside me inch by inch, "we aren't strangers anymore."

chapter
three

Rose

I REPLAYED GRANT'S WORDS TO ME AS I COWERED UNDER THE eye of Dr. McGuire, who glanced at the clock as I entered the lab. I'd made my way into his circle of candidates and cursed my stupidity for almost blowing my shot because of a one-night stand—an amazing one-night stand but a risky one.

"Whitaker, I hate to state the obvious, but you are aware this lab started an hour ago." He peered at me through the crowd of busy students as I faced him head-on.

"Yes, sir."

"And you are giving me no excuse, as well."

"I'm not good at excuses, sir. I rarely ever have to give them."

He looked over my appearance, which I was sure matched that of a sleep-deprived sex maniac. "You have less than two hours to finish this lab. Do you think you can surprise me?"

"That's one thing I am good at, sir."

I attempted to clear my mind from last night's hours of incredible sex.

And for the most part, it worked.

I aced the lab.

⁓

"Delivery, Rose," Jennifer muttered as she walked past my bedroom.

"What is it?" I squeaked, barely able to lift my head from exhaustion. I'd gone straight home after lab, scolding myself and, at the same time, replaying the previous night on repeat. If it weren't for an aching body, I wouldn't have believed it had actually happened.

"Go see for yourself," Jen muttered absently, dragging a basket of laundry past my door.

"Thanks, Jen, you are a true bitch. And thanks for letting Grant in last night while I was sleeping! What in the hell were you thinking?!" I barked at her.

"I heard you praise God all night when I got in. You're welcome, and you needed to get laid more than anyone on campus. Do tell, how was that fantastic-looking fuck stick, anyway?"

"Fuck stick?" I mumbled under my breath, still trying to find the strength to pull myself out of bed.

"He is juicy," she yelled from her bedroom.

"Yes, he is, and you are grossing me out." I pushed off my mattress with a groan, headed towards the living room, and quickly saw my delivery. There was a five-foot hoagie on the kitchen table with a message written on a napkin.

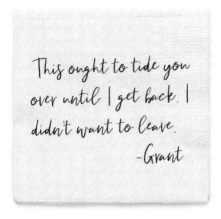

This ought to tide you over until I get back. I didn't want to leave.

-Grant

I smiled at his ridiculous gesture, then dug into the sandwich.

"I can see he clearly knows you," Jen said, snatching the napkin from my hands to read it.

"Only everything you *told* him, including our address!" I couldn't even pretend to be mad at her at that point. I'd been properly laid and was now being properly fed. "Do you want some?" I asked through a mouthful of sandwich.

"Are you going to tell me anything?"

"Nope," I said, tearing off a piece of sandwich and offering it to her.

She haphazardly fixed her copper hair into a ponytail, then cued up her iPod. She had her running clothes on and tapped her flat abdomen as she said, "Some of us can't eat like that and get away with it. I'm pressed for time, but I will be getting details. I'll see you later. Love you, bitch."

"Love you, too."

My cell phone rang, and I saw Grant's name on the caller ID. He had my address and my number.

"Smooth, Grant," I answered with a small amount of attitude.

"Rose, I can't get you out of my head. Do you miss me yet?"

I felt a tug in my chest but refused to flatter him. I was excited to hear from him but terrified at the same time. Because time was the issue, and I hoped he wasn't expecting too much from me.

"Thanks for the sandwich."

"Anything for you. Can I see you this weekend?"

I smiled at his request, though he couldn't see it. I was elated at the thought of seeing him again. I had convinced myself that it wouldn't extend beyond last night, but deep down, I hoped for more and was happy he felt the same. I paused only long enough to toy with him and not seem too eager. I wasn't sure of what I could offer, but I knew my weekend was lighter than usual. "Yeah, sure. What did you have in mind?"

"Your body, your lips, and your perfect ass."

I felt the heat radiate through me and melted into my recliner. "So, it *is* sex you're after."

"It wasn't. Now all I can think about is how you feel around me—so tight, so perfect. God, you're so beautiful. I want you so fucking bad right now. I want to lick you until you're so wet you scream for me...scream my name while I spell it out on you with my tongue."

I'd never had a man talk to me this way, and I was already on the verge of losing it. I couldn't even pretend to play coy.

"Grant," I breathed out over the phone, my chest heaving, my lower half tingling out of control.

"I'm hard as a rock. Tell me, baby, will you touch that part I want to lick so badly and tell me if it's wet?"

"Grant!" I looked around as heat crept up my face. My cheeks burned with a perfect mix of embarrassment and need.

This was a boldness I wasn't used to, and I felt the flutter rush through my every limb.

"I know it is. I'm going to push myself so far inside of you this weekend that you'll forget you ever had another lover."

I'd forgotten last night—though I hadn't bothered to tell him—that no one had ever come close to him in the bedroom. I moaned in remembrance. I couldn't help it. I knew his dirty talk was vulgar and some women would be offended by it— but I wasn't. Just thinking about his perfect hair falling over my breasts as he gazed at me, pounded into me was enough to make me do what he asked. I slid my hand down to the delicious soreness between my thighs.

"I am... wet." My voice was barely a whisper.

"Don't do anything about it. Rose, promise me you will let me take care of it."

"How long until this weekend?" I threatened with a small smile.

"Two days, but I promise it'll be worth the wait."

"Two days, Grant. The clock is ticking." I hung up with a smile on my face. He lived in Tennessee, and there was no way this could get in the way of my last semester of school.

This could be fun.

My phone rang on Friday night, and I smiled as Grant's name flashed across the screen.

"Where are you, beautiful?"

"Home. I just got out of the shower."

"Are you alone?"

I smiled and stared at my naked reflection in the mirror. I'd pampered myself with every product Jen owned. "Yes."

"Perfect, let's start right now. Go unlock your door, then get into bed."

"Grant, aren't you going to at least take me to dinner?"

"I'll take you anywhere you want. Just do it." His voice was commanding yet hopeful, and my hesitation vanished.

I walked to my front door and unlocked it, then scurried to my bedroom, still nude, and sat on the edge of the bed.

"Are you there?"

"Yes," I answered nervously.

"Lie down and close your eyes."

I heard my bedroom door open but kept my eyes closed as he'd asked me to. I listened to his voice closing in on me.

"Oh, baby, fucking beautiful," he rasped out in greeting. I heard the rustling and zip of clothes as I lay there, vulnerable, thoroughly aroused, and expectant. "You're every dream I've ever had." His first touch was a light kiss on my lips before he took my lobe between his teeth. His hands fisted in my hair, and his mouth moved in a trail over my neck and then clamped down as he sucked my skin before gently biting. I was so close that my whole body was trembling, and I cried out as he nipped at me. "Are you wet for me, Rose?"

"Grant, now. I need you now."

I didn't feel anything else until his tongue plunged deep inside of me while he simultaneously gripped underneath my thighs, pulling me to the edge of the bed. I gasped out in ecstasy as my body arched in surprise. He took my clit in his mouth, flicking his skilled tongue over it again and again until I came with a huge rush, screaming out to him, pulling his hair through my hands.

"So perfect." He dipped his fingers into me, and I began demanding the only thing that could cure my ache. "Keep them closed."

His mouth latched onto me again, every inch of my sensitive flesh already on fire.

"I can't take it," I moaned as he relentlessly assaulted me with his mouth.

I could hear the smile on his lips as he replied, "Yes, you can. You can come. I feel it...right here." I shook my head in disbelief again, shivering in delight, calling out to him. I opened my eyes and saw his gloriously naked body over mine, his eyes burning into me.

"Do you believe in love at first sight?" Without giving me a chance to answer, he took my mouth so tenderly that I had no choice but to answer with my kiss.

"Please, Grant, take me."

"I intend to, Rose. I intend to take all of you—your heart, soul, body, and mind. Even when I do have all of you, it still won't be enough."

"Why are you talking like this?" He guided himself to my entrance and pressed into me achingly slowly, stopping before giving me all of him.

"Because, Rose, I'm falling for you already, and I can't stop thinking about you, or us, or our future, or this." He buried himself inside me, and I felt the relief. My protest fled immediately.

He took me with a gentleness that made my chest tighten and resolve melt. For the first time since we'd met, I thought he might be onto something.

"Grant, I have to study. I had fun and all, but you have to go."
I tried not to make eye contact as he lay in bed next to me,
strumming his fingers over my skin.

"Fun . . ." he muttered in disbelief. I had no choice but to
look over at him.

"Fun? That was fun?" His eyebrow quirked as he waited
on me to answer, and I had to resist the urge to fill his dimple
with my tongue.

"Oh, baby, you are already hell-bent on breaking my
heart," he said playfully before tilting my chin towards him.
"This isn't just sex, Rose. I want to know you and not just in
this way. I would have waited if you hadn't attacked me, and
I still had no idea how good it felt. But now I do so . . ." His
eyebrows swept up in a double tap before his tone changed.
"Seriously, you can't kick me out. I won't let you cheapen this
to bullshit." He groaned in frustration, swiping his hand over
his face. "Fuck...I sound like a girl."

I pressed my head into my pillow, equally frustrated, before I turned to him. "Quit making this into something that
it's not. I like you. I do. I love sleeping with you, but I'm so
close to finishing school. I have to stay focused. I don't have
the time to fool around with stuff like this."

He stilled his fingers and adjusted his pillow so he was
closer to me. "Rose, this is the most important thing you'll
ever do besides being a doctor."

"And what is this again?"

"It's love, Red, or, at least, it *will* be."

I rolled my eyes as the butterflies began to circle each other
from my stomach to my chest. Looking at him made me want,

touching him made me raw, and hearing his words made me weak. Even so, the reasonable woman in me was still fighting.

"Right, Grant, and five or ten screaming orgasms constitute love?"

"No, it doesn't, and stop being so damn pessimistic. I'm not asking you to be the missus yet. I'm asking you to keep an open mind."

"I can't help it. This is crazy talk." We hadn't made it out to dinner last night, and I'd barely escaped him this morning for a shower. I thought I was home free until he whisked me back to bed. I was starving and knew I had to at least manage going over the rest of my notes for Monday's rounds.

He took my nipple in his mouth, and I let out a small cry. "Grant, I'm spent!"

"Come again, Rose." He grinned up at me as he made his way down my bare stomach and buried his head between my thighs. His tongue whispered to me, and now trained by it, I fell apart against his mouth. He grabbed the last condom from the nightstand and buried himself to the hilt as he lifted my neck to his waiting mouth.

"God." I pulled his hair hard, and he smiled at my vicious, aggravated plucking of his hair and quickly replied to it, turning me over on my hands and knees.

Every thrust was delivered without apology, and I cried out, urging him to go harder. Grant slid his hand around my hip, touching my sensitive tip, beckoning me to obey him. "Come again, and again, and again." My body replied to his order as he grunted out, shooting his heat into me and, with one last hard push, held himself there, biting into my shoulder. When we recovered, I jumped off the bed, chest heaving, and glared at him in frustration.

"Stop it! Put that damned thing away. I can't take it any-more.... Maniac!"

He laughed at my outburst, and after a short pause, I joined him in near hysterics.

He lay back on my pillow, beautifully bare, his hands be-hind his head, accentuating his bulging arms, a smug expression on his face. "I prefer insatiable, but only for you."

Blowing out a puff of air, I watched a slow smile creep across his face. Suddenly aware I was just as bared to him, his eyes roamed my body, and I could see the new naked scenarios of the two of us taking shape in his mind.

"Unh unh, nope." I put my hand up in protest before I turned and fled to my bathroom for my second shower, mak-ing sure to lock the door. I was overwhelmed, excited, and terrified because of his effect on me. It took a small eternity for me to calm myself beneath the water. I was intoxicated and definitely losing ground. He had me completely under his thumb sexually. Besides the skills I'd already shown him, my bag of tricks was empty. I'd only had a handful of sexual partners, and he was by far way more experienced than me. I was lucky that I found my sexuality young and could bring myself to orgasm, but this man could do it with so much ease that it frightened me. Experience or not, I seemed to have the same effect on him.

I felt the soreness between my legs and vowed to give myself a break. The thought of his tongue on me led my lower half to protest, and I immediately found myself wanting him again. I threw an all-out fit, scrubbing my body with exfoliant and shaving my legs. He had to go. He was in my head, under my skin, and merciless in the bedroom. I had a goal to meet, a fellowship to earn. I needed all my wits about me, and he was fucking them into oblivion.

I found him in my kitchen with breakfast made. He pulled out the seat for me as I gave him a wary look.

"You aren't leaving?" I tried to ignore the hurt look on his face, though it pained me to see it.

He brushed off my rude comment as he kissed my cheek. "We'll go to my land. You can study there."

"I will not. I can study just fine here."

"Come on, Rose, all I'm asking for is a day. I won't distract you. I will keep my hands to myself. I have to leave again soon."

"Fine," I said, forking a bite of omelet. "You made me breakfast, so I'll give you one day. Then you'll leave." I met his eyes and saw another hint of sadness as I picked up a piece of toast.

"You'd think you'd be in a better mood with all the good stuff I just gave you."

I grinned at my plate, then at him. "I'm exhausted. I've never had this much sex in my life."

"And you never will again with anyone else. Eat before it gets cold. I'm going to grab a shower if that's okay." I nodded and waved off his kiss, still a little frustrated.

Focus, Rose.

Now get up and get into the shower with him.

Damn it!

I'm not the kind of woman who throws out years of hard work for a man and never would be. I knew I was treading a fine line. Although I was ahead in my curriculum—because that was where I felt secure and comfortable—Grant put me at risk of losing that safety. I could easily get lost in him sexually.

I already had. The whole situation made no sense. But why did it have to? I was having fun. I'd earned it.

No more debate. Just go with it.

However, I refused to just go with it. I'd worked too damn hard. I drummed up some strict rules as I sat there eating my breakfast, baffled at how 'take charge' he'd been since that first night. I had given him way too much leeway, and now it seemed I was paying for it. I would have my fun, but I would have to make a few things clear today.

Resolute and satisfied, I dressed in shorts and a simple white tee, then laughed when he exited the bathroom in the same outfit.

"Great minds," he muttered.

"Yeah, great minds. Let's go, Grant. Daylight is wasting." He leaned in to kiss me, and I put my entire hand over his mouth.

"Just a break is all I'm asking."

He nodded and turned my hips, holding them while walking behind me in the hall. "You do know that people have the weekends off for a reason." I shivered at his breath on my neck.

"If this is the way we are starting the day, I'm not going."

He pulled the front door open as I grabbed my purse and keys, then turned to him.

"I can see how important this is to you. I won't say another word about it." He seemed sincere, and I nodded as I walked past him.

He lifted me into the passenger side of his monstrous black truck and kissed my hand before he shut the door. I found myself looking for him in the rearview mirror as he made his way to the driver's side. It was hot, sweltering. I looked at the thermostat as he cranked the car and saw it was nearing one hundred and six degrees. That was Texas in August for you. Grant scanned me as he started the truck and saw I was melting in my seat. I felt the air come on and tilted my head back, exposing my neck in anticipation of the relief that was coming, but to my horror, I felt the heater on full blast.

"Grant, what in the hell are you doing!" I heard him chuckle as the heat began to blow on my face, and I was instantly drenched in sweat. The blood in my head began to boil as he turned on the radio, ignoring my fervent pleas to turn on the air. I leaned in to change the air, and he swatted my hand away with a scolding, "No!"

After another minute of melting into his leather seat, I look at him incredulously.

"What?" He was laughing hysterically at my reaction until I started to open my door at a stop light. He reached over and pulled the door closed, still smiling as he consoled me. "Okay, baby...now it gets wonderful."

He turned on the air conditioner, and the ice-cold air hit me and took away my itch to escape the truck. He turned onto the highway, hitting the gas hard, and cracked his windows, allowing the heat to make its way out the window.

"Ahhh." I sank into my seat, enjoying the comfort of the air. Still a bit furious with his bullshit stunt, I looked over at him as he continued to laugh silently.

"You're a mean bastard," I said with a grudging smile.

He turned to me with what I knew now was his signature wink. "You're it for me, Rose."

"Back to this again, huh? Stop being such a moron."

"I'll prove it."

"Okay, Grant, just take me to study."

After my statement, I realized that I'd left the book I

needed *and* my tablet back at my apartment. How in the hell had I managed that after protesting so profusely!? I'd left the one thing I needed the most. I demanded that he take me back, but he refused, stating that I needed a break.

"You want me to be in this *fling* with you, and you are ruining it already by keeping me from my books!" I saw him flinch at the word fling and felt guilty at my word choice.

"You need this. Give me one day. I didn't forget your books. You did."

"You're right, you didn't, but, Grant—"

"But shit, shut up and have fun with me, Rose." He pulled up to a gas station and jumped out of the truck to escape my reply. I laughed at his boldness. This guy clearly didn't have a clue who he was talking to. When he emerged from the store, his eyes found mine through the windshield, and I could see they were asking me, not telling me. When he opened the door and made himself comfortable, I let him off the hook.

"Fine," I said when he started the truck.

He leaned in and gave me a soft kiss. "Thanks, you won't regret it."

I reasoned my way into a day of fun with the most amazing sex partner and super sexy man I'd ever met. I took in his features as he smiled heavily all the way to the gate of his land. I hadn't noticed it on our first night, but the gate ran a great length across several different pastures. It was way more than I'd seen on our previous trip. There were fields and fields of undeveloped land, and we were completely secluded. Trees lined the outer banks of the gate, and only a few were visible within them. We pulled up to the most shaded area, and I saw the pond a great distance ahead of us.

"How much do you own?"

"All of it. As far as you can see."

"It's amazing."

"Glad you like it because we're going to build our house today, Rose."

"What? I'm not qualified to do that!"

"Neither am I. We're just daydreaming here." He jumped out of the truck again before I could say another word but caught my eyes before he closed the door.

Looking around at the property, I saw the happiness cover his features as he unpacked his truck, took out a huge yellow island-sized float, and hooked it up to a small air pump.

"Do you need any help?" I asked as he smoothed out the wrinkled edges of the float.

"Nope, I've got this. Make yourself comfortable," he said, dumping ice into a cooler packed with beer.

"I have no suit."

He didn't hesitate before gracing me with his dimple. "Your bra and panties will do."

"You could've asked me to bring one," I said grudgingly.

"I hadn't planned on it being this easy, but you surprised me again."

"Well, to hell with your presumptions, Grant. I'd be more comfortable in a suit," I ranted, growing impatient with his ready-made plans. I was becoming a sucker for him more and more by the minute.

"Oh, baby, you're making me hard." He teased as he eyed me over the enormous and growing float.

"You are *crazy!*" I declared with the lift of my voice.

"Crazy about the most beautiful woman in Texas."

"Hardly." I rolled my eyes and absently ran my hand

through the rat's nest on top of my head, trying to separate my curls.

"I've searched for you high and low."

"Liar, you were with that girl when you met me."

"I was with that girl for a good six months before I met you." Shock washed over me as I realized this was all getting to be too much.

"You dumped your long-time girlfriend!"

"Yes, my plan was to break up with her. I went there for that purpose, and I saw you. It was fate if you ask me. And six months is not long-term and doesn't even compare to the time we will be sharing."

"It's just so easy, huh? Move on to the next one? What does that say about you?" I put my hands on my hips, thinking of my old hurt caused by David and how easily he'd pushed me aside after four long years together.

"It says I knew I was wasting my time with her. Stop being so dramatic. She and I were just another in-between. You know what those are? The 'in-betweens' to get to the good one."

"Wow, poor girl. She must be heartbroken."

"She wasn't happy, but I don't think she was completely faithful, either."

"What do you mean?"

"I told you my schedule is crazy."

"Yeah, so?"

"Well, the last time I showed up late at her house, I found men's boxers and an electric razor. She claimed her dad left them when he visited. I seriously doubt her dad wears Armani boxers. Even if he did, why in the hell would he leave them at his daughter's apartment? It was going nowhere. I wanted to end it then, but I got called back to Tennessee because of an emergency, so I waited until I could come down again. I'm not the type of guy that can do that shit by phone or text. It's just not me."

"So why were you at our lecture?"

"She was nervous. She'd heard about what a hardass the doctor was, and she wanted me there. I had no intention of staying until I saw you." He popped a beer and hung his head as he looked at me. "Rose, listen to me, hear me. It's over with her, and you have no reason to feel guilty, and I sure as hell don't. My heart wasn't in it." He turned on his portable speaker, and I heard country music reverberate across the pond.

"Oh, hell no. Better find something else," I said with a laugh. When it came to music, I was a snob of sorts, and country was out of the question.

"It's my taste, and I love it. Get used to it."

"I most certainly will not!" I stated as he gave me a wink as he closed the cap to the now fully-inflated float before tossing it onto the ground. "You're involved with a true Texan, kid. Deal with it."

I rolled my eyes as he took a bag of weed from his pocket and began to roll a joint on the hood of his car. I looked around as if the police would be running up to us at any minute.

I lifted my brow at his new chore. "Don't expect me to smoke that with you, stoner cowboy."

"It might do you a world of wonder...Doctor."

"I've tried it. Not for me. No one smokes pot past the age of twenty-five anymore, Grant."

His brow crested high at my statement. "Bullshit."

"Look, I don't condemn or condone, okay. Do what you want." I circled around the huge float between us, then grabbed a beer, downing it in seconds.

He eyed me as he twisted the last of his joint. "Like I said, it's my only vice, aside from my newly formed addiction of living between your thighs. So, if it bothers you that much, I won't."

"No, it really doesn't," I replied before I quirked a grin up at him. "Do your thing."

He stripped down to his briefs, and I felt my body grow weak at the sight of him. He was perfectly built. He had a long torso, and I could see every single muscle etched into him. His broad chest was sprinkled with dark hair, a string of tree branch tattoos that cascaded down his right forearm, and a wicked-looking Cheshire cat on his shoulder. I loved tracing those branches as he hovered over me.

"Strip, beautiful. You're safe here. There's no one around." He gave me a wicked grin that rivaled the cat on his arm before his next offering. "I bought sunblock. It's in the bag in the front seat." He took off with the float and placed it on the shallow bank in the water. I grabbed the bag from the seat, smiling as I noticed the rest of its contents. I opened the box, tucked two condoms into the padding of my bra, and hid the rest in the cab of the truck. Safe was an illusion with Grant around. The man had one hell of a sexual appetite.

Who's got the power now, Tarzan? Jane does, that's who.

I took off my clothes, thankful to be at least matching in my hot pink bra and panty set. I covered my body in the sunblock and whipped my head down when I felt Grant rubbing the excess onto my legs.

"Rose," he breathed heavily, looking up at me, his eyes asking me...*something.*

"Grant," I whispered breathlessly as he kneeled before me.

His blue eyes looked up at me with so much need that I was instantly raw. The look he gave me was sincere and desperate.

He licked me through my panties, and I began panting as I felt the tug coming for me. "I crave this now," he said, moving my panties to the side and flicking his tongue across my waiting center. "Licking—" flick "—you—" flick "—I could dine on this alone and sustain—" flick, flick, flick. I put my hands on his shoulders, letting him have his way. He slipped his fingers inside me gently while remaining on his knees. I felt his tongue explore me at my entrance, where it met his fingers and leaned into his kiss. He only toyed with me, leaving me close to the edge but never pushing me over.

"It's you." He lifted off his knees and planted a gentle kiss on my lips, then backed away, paralyzing me with his eyes but gripping me to him. "It's definitely you." I felt the words hit me deeply and closed my eyes in unison with him as our lips met in a soft kiss. He dipped his tongue in, coaxing mine into a dizzying dance, and I felt a moan escape my throat. He pulled away again, and my heart skipped, on the verge of believing that he did feel for me.

I pulled him to me and jumped up to wrap my legs around him. He caught me and cupped my ass, holding me tightly to him as he searched my eyes. I leaned in slowly, kissed him this time with my own brand of gentleness, and watched his amazed expression when I pulled away. My lips shook again, very much like they did before our first kiss, and I heard my heart pounding in my ears. It was an addictive rush, more than just attraction, more than what I'd labeled this whole situation. It was just...*more*. I went in again, unable to get enough. They were nothing like the kisses we had shared last night. It was... different. I dropped my legs as he pulled me into him again.

It was as if we were fighting without saying a word. His kiss ran through me, weakening my knees, and they buckled as he gripped me tighter, letting me know he had me. And with that kiss, he did.

He pulled back but kept my gaze, and I stumbled forward into his chest. He smiled and nodded as if to confirm what had just happened. I simply stood looking up at him with fresh eyes while my heart banged against my chest.

"Ready to have some fun?"

I nodded in bewilderment as he scooped me up into both arms and sat me in the huge float at the edge of the pond. He pulled the cooler in and grabbed a few towels.

I sat in a daze, staring at him as he paddled us to the center of the pond.

I can't love him already, and he can't love me. That's insane.

No way. He can't love me. This can't be real. I dismissed it all, chalking it up to being *without* for way too long. I wouldn't go another year without sex. Apparently, it made a person delusional.

"Is it as pretty in the day as it is at night, Rose?" I nodded furiously, not taking my eyes off him. He chuckled in delight and surprise as we both realized I was in no way referring to the land. His hair was perfectly straight but was so thick it feathered on each side of his chin as he tilted his head while rowing with the small plastic paddles, leading us further into the pond. He pulled in the oars and plucked a beer from the cooler as I sat back, taking in the sun. I smiled and closed my eyes, thankful for being forced to have a day off.

"Tell me what you want, Rose."

"Another beer," I chuckled, holding my hand out and meeting his gaze.

"I'm serious. What do you see happening...you know, in the future?" He lit his joint and began smoking it as casually as one would smoke a cigarette. I laughed as he coughed through his first drag.

"It's really hard to take you seriously when you're smoking that stuff."

"It's not mind-altering, baby. It relaxes me. I...um, need this more than you could ever know." He paused briefly before he looked up, admitting, "I'm afraid to hit the bottle when I need to relax or take the edge off. My dad...well, he was a real bastard when he was on the bottle, and I don't want to end up like him. I don't want to depend on anything, really, but it's just been so fucking hard these last few years...just...hard." His face went a little dark, so I gave him an honest answer and a subject change.

"My sister and I want to start our own practice."

He smirked a little, seemingly happy with my reply. "What else," he prodded, tapping his ash into the water.

"I haven't thought that far ahead."

"Bullshit." He coughed again, and I could clearly see the hard line in his shoulders disappear.

"Wow, that must be some good stuff."

"It is." He nodded. "Tell me what you want."

"I want the life of an accomplished surgeon."

"You can do that all on your own."

"I don't need anything else." I was tempted to tell him then that I was a born romantic and wanted a fairytale romance that led to a happy ending with beautiful children and toasts on every anniversary—and then some. But as many premature overtures as he'd made, I still didn't feel comfortable confessing it to him...yet.

He cracked open a beer and handed it to me. I enjoyed the cold liquid as it went down my throat and sunk further into the cushion of the seats that held us upright and facing each other.

"Rose, you will be an accomplished surgeon. There's got to be something else that you want for your life. Don't you want more?"

And just as I'd convinced myself I wouldn't confess what my heart held sacred, I caved. "I want what my parents have."

"Your parents?"

"They are my ideal. I look at them and see so much love on their faces. It's one of those things you have to see to understand. They could be in a full-blown, raging fight, and you can still tell they are ridiculously in love and have been since they met in their twenties. It's amazing what they have. I don't expect that for myself, but if you want to know what I really want—it's that. It's an unrealistic standard." I shrugged my shoulders, and he leaned in.

"Done."

"You can't really think that about us."

"Why not? You aren't as smart as you think you are in *this* sense, Rose. You might be a brilliant doctor, but I know better when it comes to *this*."

I shook my head in argument. "Why are you so intent on forever with me?"

He looked at his lap on an exhale before he turned his heavy gaze to me. "Because that's what my heart told me the second I looked at you. And for the first time in my life, I'm letting it lead the way."

He didn't give me a chance to absorb or respond before he started rattling off his house plans. "So, I figure we will build the house, a one-story where the shed sits. A huge, one-story ranch, what do you think?"

I burst out in laughter as he carried on with his mindset without so much as pausing. "It's your house."

"Indulge me," he challenged, exhaling a puff of smoke. There was something so alluring about him at that moment that it took me a second to find words.

I scanned the lot and realized the shed was the perfect place to start. There were a few trees cascading over the pond and more than an acre or two behind the shed.

"Behind the tree line, a large ranch, huge kitchen and living space, large bathrooms are a must. At least five bedrooms and a study so I can read."

"What else," he urged as he listened intently.

"No pool, just a huge dock for fishing and swimming."

"My thoughts exactly. Keep going."

"No pets except for these." I pointed to the ducks circling our float and laughed as Grant had to swat one away to keep it from snatching the joint from his fingers. He took the last of it in his lungs and threw it over as I swallowed another sip of beer, getting lost in my imagination.

"A fireplace—three of them, in fact—one in my study, one in the bedroom, and family room, and they have to be stone and very large."

"Done. What else?" He was quickly becoming excited with each word I spoke, and I felt myself growing more involved in his game than I intended.

"An arboretum around the tree here with comfortable, oversized chairs. It has to lead to a huge patio with a stone fire pit and grill. And a matching stone waterfall."

"Where is all this coming from?"

"My dad is an architect." He sat straight up in his inflatable seat and gave me a million-dollar smile.

"No wonder you're so thorough. You must've grown up in some house."

"I did. It's the most amazing house, really. Yours will be amazing, too."

"Sounds like it. You need more sunblock."

He grabbed the bottle, made his way toward me, and began to rub it on my shoulders. I closed my eyes at the feel of his fingertips on my skin.

"It will be exactly what you want. When can I meet your dad?"

I jerked out of my daze and met his eyes.

"Absolutely not!"

"Why? I'll be a perfect gentleman, I promise."

"Look . . ." I pushed him away and grabbed the bottle, rubbing the rest of what he'd left into my thighs and stomach. "This was just for fun. I don't even know your last name, let alone know you well enough to take you home to my parents."

"Foster is my last name. What else do you want to know, Rose Whitaker, with two siblings and two living parents that have been married for almost thirty years? You'll graduate with your doctorate in medicine in December. You've only loved one guy, and he cheated on you your first year of med school with—" he paused, making quotation marks with his hands "—'that skank Marie Johnson,' whom he married and has two kids with. You hate soggy cereal and people who scrape their teeth against their fork. You need more sex in your life, and you need me."

I sat back in the float with what I was sure was a gaping mouth and a question in my eyes.

"Jennifer is all about cold hard cash."

"Ask *me*! Don't go digging around in my personal life, asking questions that no one has a right to know unless I want them to. Ask me." I was furious, though I knew the main reason was because he brought up my ex. It wasn't that it still bothered me about his cheating. It bothered me that *Grant* knew he cheated on me, but I wasn't sure why.

"I'm sorry." He passed his beer from one hand to the other, looking down at it, refusing to meet my hostile eyes.

"You should be. Now you will answer everything I ask."

"Fine, shoot."

"Why is this thing between us so important to you?"

"When I saw you, I knew you were the only thing that could make life bearable again. I have no brothers or sisters, and all my friends are married with kids or are relentless bachelors. I don't want that to be me. Not anymore. I can't explain it any better. I knew I was just bullshitting with Rebecca, and I—"

"What? Her name is Rebecca?"

"Yeah, why?"

I wanted to flee but had nowhere to go. I was trapped on the pond with him, and I was suddenly terrified. I knew better than to believe this was just a coincidence. My mom had been pointing signs out to me my whole life, and my dad wholeheartedly agreed with every single one. I had dismissed their belief in fate at times, as it was too unrealistic for me.

"What's the matter, Rose? I'm sorry I talked about Rebecca. I told you—"

"Don't. Don't say that name." Rebecca was the name of the woman that drove a wedge between my parents and is the mother of my half-brother, Paul. My mom had fled Texas after my dad had broken her heart badly, and he had married

Rebecca. My parents reconciled fourteen years after my mom left during a chance meeting at a motel she once owned. There were an incredible amount of signs that led them back to one another. The story, though I believed every bit of it, was unbelievable. Against all odds, they had found and kept their happiness for all these years.

I looked to Grant, who was eyeing me suspiciously. "You believe in it, too."

"In *what!*" I was becoming hysterical with each passing second. Downing my beer, I got up to jump in the pond.

"Rose, don't freak. It's okay. Just talk it out with me."

"It's nothing but a huge coincidence, Grant."

"What is?"

"I don't want to talk about it." I dove in and felt the cold water take away the heat from my limbs. When I surfaced, I exhaled and slowly let my good sense fall back into play. It was just a coincidence. Nothing could possibly ever be this cut and dry. "God, this feels unbelievable," I murmured, sifting the water through my hands.

I heard the water splash next to me and felt his arms come around me as I cleared my eyes.

"I love it here, and you feel unbelievable."

"Grant, this—you and me—it's too fast, too much. Are you trying to scare me away?"

"I'm more scared of not saying how I feel, of not telling you I want you, of not taking the chance with you, and begging you for the same."

"God, that's some amazing line."

"I want you," he said as water cascaded around his perfect features. "I've had enough years of doing the wrong shit and being with the wrong women. I took one look at you, and a thousand memories we hadn't made hit me in waves. I can't explain it, and it may seem fast to you, but to me, it's as natural as taking my next breath. Maybe I'm full of shit. Maybe you'll prove me wrong—but so far, everything inside me says that the minute I saw you, I was done with the unknown, and my life had just started. Call it impulse and heartbeat in tune for the first fucking time in my life. I'm going after something I feel in my gut is right."

He pulled away from me, the sudden absence of his warmth all too noticeable. He watched me for a beat and then submerged himself under the water before he pulled himself back onto the float. He resumed his seat, popping another beer as I noticed his jawline harden, but I refused to cater to his tantrum. This was too much, and it was ridiculous for him to think I would just go along without thinking it through or getting to know him better.

"I'm not giving up," he said, cutting his eyes at me as I remained in the water. "I might be a little ticked off with myself right now—bearing my soul to you like this, saying all these things I never thought I would say to a woman and making a damn fool of myself—but I'm not giving up."

"I don't know what to say, Grant."

"Stay with me, here, today. That's enough."

I pulled myself onto the island in the center of the pond. Soon after, we dropped the serious discussion and began splashing around with the ducks and at each other. We argued over the radio as I switched it to a rap station. Grant protested profusely until I started rapping to him, fully involved with arms and the swivel of my hips, keeping him entertained. An hour later, the sun began to drop behind us, and I was buzzing heavily as my eyes started to follow Grant's every move. I could feel my hunger building as he spoke about his home in Tennessee and how he couldn't wait to be back in Texas permanently. In exchange, I told him stories about Dallas and me and the torture we put our parents through growing up. He listened attentively and laughed as I told him about the first time Dallas and I got drunk together.

"So, we pull up to the drive-through window, and the shots we'd just had suddenly hit us *hard*."

"Drinking and driving?" Grant said with an authoritative tone.

"*Actually*, Judgey McJudgerson," I growled out as a slow smile spread across his face, "we didn't make it that far. The drive-through was in the same shopping center as the bar. So, yes, I drove drunk all of six feet at about two miles per hour. Are you going to let me tell you this story?"

"Go on then, baby," he urged in a thick southern drawl, lifting a beer to his lips with a grin.

"Anyway, we were hysterical by the time we made it to the window, and I actually passed it as it opened, and the guy there was set to greet us. He caught on to us immediately as I stuck the car in reverse and had to back up to reach the window. Dallas was laughing so hard she peed her pants right there. I was trying my best to console the guy in the drive-through as he voiced his concern for our safety. Anyway, I had already decided to park and call a cab after we got our food, but before we pulled away, the guy at the window had to make sure he voiced his concern again. 'Ladies, are you sure you're okay to drive?' I lifted my hand and waved him off with an 'Oh, we're fine. Really, don't worry.' And just as I said it . . ." I paused my story as I snorted, ". . . I put my foot on the gas, and we went backward! I'd never taken the car out of reverse!" I started howling as I recalled the look of sheer terror on the man's face. "There was no one behind us, thank God, or it would have been worse. And I *did* park right then and called a cab while Mrs. Pissed Pants ate my food and hers." Grant was eyeing me with a huge grin on his face. "But that's us, you know. That's how we are. It was my twenty-first birthday, and my sister got drunker than I did. And before you lecture me, I haven't had a sip and got behind the wheel since." Grant nodded as he looked at me, still chuckling.

"We are nothing but trouble when we're together, but we can't do a damn thing without the other. She and I are like fraternal twins with a bigger age difference. We just don't work or feel right without the other. That's the way it's always been. What sweetens our future is that we're going to build something together." I looked up to see Grant watching me. I felt goosebumps spread across my skin and let out all my air. God, he was beautiful. I tried to hide how much he was affecting me as I went on. "They named her Dallas because my mom hated the city. Well, and this state. After what she and my dad went through to be together, Dallas is what sealed the deal... the city, not the sister."

Good Lord, captain obvious, could you sound any more ridiculous? God, am I drunk now? I'm totally babbling, and he's letting me.

"They named me Rose due to my mom's love of her yellow roses. She has this fantastic garden filled with them. And the yellow rose is ironically our state flower, did you know that? Don't take my beer away."

Grant burst out laughing as he nodded at my half-empty beer and gave me a wink. "I won't take that one, I promise."

Our eyes danced over each other as he spoke next. "The only person I was ever that close with was my dad," he said softly. "So, I get it. I do." He told me how, at age six, he started working on planes at an airstrip close to his dad's house. His dad couldn't afford daycare, and his mom had just left them, so he brought Grant to work with him every day. I watched him as he animatedly told me the story of the first time he flew with his dad. Unable to control myself any longer, as I watched Grant's lips move and consumed by hunger for him, I stopped him mid-sentence when I unhooked my bra and let it fall. The condoms I'd forgotten I had stashed in my bra hit the floor. He lifted his brow in amusement until he saw my panties fly through the air before smacking him in the chest.

I could feel the sunburn on my shoulders but ignored it. I was hungry, and he was the solution. Leaning back against the edge of the float, I dipped my head in the water, wetting my hair, then smoothed my hands over it. He watched the water cascade over my nipples, which were already hard in anticipation.

In response, Grant pushed his briefs down, revealing his mouth-watering erection. With hungry eyes, he stroked himself a few times, looking at me naked in front of him.

"Do it again," I ordered, watching him close his eyes as he took himself in his hand, stroked again, and let go. He grabbed a condom off the floor wordlessly, except for the eye fucking, and tore it with his teeth. I watched him slide it on, my center aching to be filled. "When I come inside you this time, I'm making you mine."

Eyes locked, I made my way to him, kneeling and naked as the setting sun pierced through the trees behind him. He placed his hand behind my neck, pulling me in. I licked my lips and met his kiss. It was slow and sweet. He pulled me away gently, his fist twisted in my hair as he spoke.

"Rose, maybe you've convinced yourself you're incapable of love right now, or even worse, not worthy of it. Don't let one dickhead cheat you out of what every single person on earth deserves."

"And what's that?" I whispered, completely leveled by his kiss.

"Love, baby, love. It's your time to be loved, and I'm the one who's going to do it."

"Please, Grant, give me time to—"

"I'll give you whatever you want."

He cut me with his gentle words, sincerity filtering through his eyes. Loving hands brought my hips down over him, and I gasped in pleasure, wrapping my arms around his neck. I moaned his name over and over between strokes as he tugged at my hair, kissing me thoroughly. He stopped his thrusts to rub me back and forth over him, working himself deeper inside. Our kiss morphed into something else entirely. Our carnal touches turned tender. I lifted myself slowly above him and gently let myself down, feeling every inch of him. Closing my eyes, he stroked my face with his fingertips and kissed my forehead. I reopened them, suddenly emboldened by our connection, and drank his blue eyes in as I took another slow plunge on top of him. He was throbbing and so deep. I lingered above him, riding him slowly. A cry of defeat escaped my lips, and a wave of emotion washed over me as I came, shattering around him. I held his eyes as he pulled me into another deep kiss. My heart soared as he whispered to me, his intent clear, "It's you, baby. I know it is. Just take it, and I'm yours." He came then and buried his head in my chest, wrapping his arms around me, holding me tight against him. I felt the dam burst and realized I'd been in over my head since the minute I'd laid eyes on him.

"I'll take it, Grant." I tilted my head down to get a look at his face still buried in my chest, and saw his hidden smile. He rose to his knees with me still wrapped around him and laid me beneath him. It was the first time I realized the true meaning of making love because that's exactly what we were doing.

chapter
four

Rose

YOU KNOW THOSE STORIES? THE ONES WHERE THE COUPLE meets, and they marry days later and remain married for sixty-something years? I've always been a fan of those stories. I mean, I'm not naïve enough to believe that a good majority of those weren't shotgun weddings due to a soldier leaving for war or a woman suddenly in the family way. The notion seemed so damned old-fashioned now, and my generation is so quick to divorce these days. Those stories become less and less and are considered a Hollywood-type marriage, meaning the time frame from beginning to end spans the length of time it takes for the two actors to fall in love, marry, shoot the movie, and divorce by release day.

The question I'd been asking myself repeatedly—when I wasn't mind-deep into labs—was I Hollywood or old-fashioned? My parents fell in love in a month, or at least that's how they explained it. In all honesty, I never in a million years thought it was possible for me. I credited myself with a level head, and as I sat surrounded by books, I was sure it was still on straight. I hadn't missed a single class, rotation, or lab.

But I wanted—no, I *needed* this thing with Grant to work

because after only three weeks, what I felt was not just lust, and it was far more than affection. I had nobody to prove anything to aside from myself. I wanted to believe he was sincere in his sudden feelings for me. I wanted more than anything to believe that it wasn't just fantastic sex—which was in a category of its own—that kept my mind occupied with thoughts of him and that damned house I'd help build in my mind. Because if I had to visualize the rest of my life, that's exactly what I would picture. And he is exactly the type of man I would want to spend it with, given he didn't have an ugly head yet to rear. But was that really my fear? It didn't seem possible for Grant to have a Hyde. He was warm, caring, and doting and seemed hell-bent on pleasing me. I was hesitant about going along with his whole 'love at first sight' scenario. Like, for some reason, I would need to justify it to myself when all it did was cheapen the authenticity of it. I mean, wasn't that the point? And as if he'd read my mind, my phone rattled with a message.

> **Grant: I'm working on this plane, and I keep thinking I'll own it one day. What do you think about flying everywhere together?**

> **Rose: I think it would be a dream. Seriously, you're a pilot, too?**

> **Grant: Of course. But I won't mention the mile-high club. That would be cheesy.**

Ten seconds later...

> **Grant: Would you like to join the mile-high club?**

I laughed loudly as he continued his rant. I found he did

that a lot. Especially when I was studying or in class and was slow to answer a text.

Grant: Of course, that is unless you're already a member. Then don't tell me. Fuck. I would hate that. Okay, now you have to tell me. Baby, you there?

Rose: I'm here.

Grant: Well, are you going to tell me?

Rose: No.

Grant: That's just cruel. Don't forget you're a screamer.

Rose: No I'm not.

Grant: Not yet.

Rose: Is that a threat?

Grant: I have moves you haven't had yet, baby, and I will have you screaming on a plane. Now send me a naughty picture to get me through the day.

Rose: You're so random, and hell no.

Grant: Chicken.

Rose: No way, you have no idea how many channels it has to go through to get to you.

Grant: Give me something.

Rose: No.

Grant: Prude.

Rose: Pervert.

Grant: I'm waiting.

Rose: Hold your breath, too, you ass.

Grant: God, I miss you. Now I'm hard. I love it when you get feisty. Where are you?

Rose: Home

Grant: Perfect. Pull down your panties and show me where you want me.

Burning was all I could feel as my pulse kicked into overdrive. The way he felt inside me when he swiveled his hips and hit *that* spot was all I could think about. Now I was aching deep inside, a part that only Grant had touched, only Grant could seem to fill.

Becoming bold with thoughts of him and the way he made me feel, I slid my panties off and went to the bathroom. Ten minutes later, I was sweating as I contorted my body at every odd angle, trying to capture a decent naked picture of myself. With my foot propped on the counter, I was just about to snap a money shot, or so I thought, when a door smacked painfully into my side, sending me flying through the air. I landed on the toilet, my phone escaping my hand only to fall dead center of the throne with a loud plunk.

"Jennifer!" I shrieked, looking at my ruined phone, then reached for a towel above me that was hanging on the rack.

Jennifer stood silent for all of the three seconds it took to assess the situation before she immediately sat on her ass at the bathroom doorway, erupting in hysterical laughter.

Neither of us really had any body shame and had seen each other naked a hundred times, but this was different entirely. I buried my head in my hands and shook it back and forth in embarrassment. I'd never been that 'sexy' girl, and trying had turned into a disaster.

"Okay...so," Jennifer started in an attempt to soothe me. Her cackling ceased temporarily, but her shit-eating grin remained. "I guess every woman gets curious to see her goods at least once."

"It's not that," I said, my face flaming slightly. "I was trying to get a sexy shot for Grant."

Jen looked at me for a split second before bursting into more laughter. "Rose, and you thought taking a shot from underneath would be the best plan? Oh, buddy." She laughed. "No, no, no. Flat on your back, legs spread, and with way better lighting. You want my selfie stick?"

I pursed my lips, wrapping the towel firmly around me. "Such an expert."

"I'm in a long-distance relationship so, yes, I am somewhat." She stood and looked me over. "You've got it bad for him, and before you protest, that's a good thing. I like Grant for you. I got to know him before deciding he could have you."

"You could have told *me*," I said, grabbing a plastic bag from underneath the sink and using it to wrap my hand so I could fish my phone out of the toilet.

"I just did," she said with a grin. "I fucking hate what David did to you and—"

"Dead horse, Jennifer, and this is not about David or

getting over him. That's over, been over," I cut her off. "This is about Grant, and this is *way* different. I can be one hundred percent me when I'm with him, and he seems to accept me."

She nodded as I brushed past her. "I'm happy for you, Rose." She followed me into my bedroom, where I dressed in preparation to go buy a new phone.

"It's just shitty timing because I want that damned spot under McGuire, you know. I know that's all I need to concentrate on, but now I want him, too. He's agreed to take a back seat to school, but I don't know how long it will last. My schedule will only become more demanding."

Jen sat on the edge of my bed. "The man for you will wait as long as it takes. Look at me and Alex. We haven't seen each other in two months, but we do the work, and the wait is almost over." Her voice shook as she looked up at me, happiness and excitement seeping out of her every pore. "God, just thinking about the next few months makes me fucking... giddy," she piped, teary-eyed.

"You two give me hope," I said, grabbing my keys.

"Where are you going?"

"To get a phone not covered in a death strain." I winked. "And you can leave your selfie stick on my bed."

She chuckled as she followed me out. "Thatta girl. And remember good lighting and use a soft filter."

"I think I'm falling for him," I said, pausing at the front door and turning to look for her reaction. "And I'm not doing a damn thing to stop it."

Jen simply nodded, taking her seat on our ancient blue couch and opening her laptop before pausing to look up at me. "I've got your back."

"Love you, bitch," I said before making my way out the door.

"Just remember to give credit where credit is due," she called after me before I closed the door. I made it two steps before I heard her again. "You know when you two decide to name your kids!"

⁓

I practically skipped to my car in light of her support and the realization that I may—for the first time in years—be in love. I wanted to call my sister and tell her, but I was already afraid of an adverse reaction. Dallas hadn't been a fan of anything love related in some seriously long years. She'd had one love, her ex, Dean, and like my own experience, it had turned out just as bad. I couldn't even begin to imagine the crap she would give me if she knew I had fallen in love with a man in mere weeks. So, on the trip to town, when I asked myself whether Grant and I could fall in love in the blink of an eye and live that way forever, I was sure—like everything else Grant had predicted—he could make it true. We, *together*, could make it true.

It would be our story. We would have one of *those,* and it would start with him declaring to me within five minutes of meeting that I would become his wife.

So instead of calling my sister, I purchased a new phone, and when Grant sent his next text, I sent him one in return. It was a picture of a woman, hopeful of falling in love and completely bared to him, both in body and soul. I could see my vulnerability when I studied it. I could see the hope in my eyes and the flush of my body. I could also see my confidence, and for the first time in a long time, I wasn't ashamed of the manicured woman I wasn't. I was proud of the woman I was. Whatever high I was on was due to his affection for me, and I knew it wasn't going to end anytime soon. So, with my mind and heart in agreement, I jumped in with both feet.

I felt her nails dig into my arm before I saw Rebecca's face. "You bitch, what did you say to my boyfriend?" she hissed, pulling me to her and taking me away from the deli line at *The Bistro*.

"Take your hands off me, or so help me. We won't be talking." I was way too old for this shit and knew better than to threaten an angry bee, but I stood my ground. I had the strength of an eighty-year-old woman, but I could bark like a scary Chihuahua.

"We had a good thing going, then you come along, and he won't even talk to me!"

"Let me make this perfectly clear: *he* came to *me*. I did nothing," I said, darting my eyes around to see who was watching.

"You did something," she snapped, crossing her arms.

"I can't help what he did to you, and I'm sorry, really. I know how that can hurt, but I did nothing to start this."

"I don't believe you. He was going to marry me."

"Did he tell you that?" I felt a tug of jealousy at the thought.

"No, but it was coming."

"He made his decision, and I ask that you respect it and our relationship." Clearly, this wasn't the right thing to say as I watched her eyes bulge.

"Your relationship?"

"Yes, we are seriously involved now. I'm sorry if that hurts you, but it's the truth." I shrugged my shoulders as she took in the yoga pants and T-shirt I was wearing.

"You aren't even pretty enough for him!"

"Thanks," I snapped, then resumed picking out my lunch.

"He will be back," she said with false confidence. "I know it. He couldn't get enough of me, and you're just a whim."

"I am the whim he is coming to see tonight!" I seethed, facing her with my full bitch on.

"Bitch, watch your back."

"Watch my back? What are you, ten? Look, I love Grant. He's an awesome guy, and I'm sorry you're hurting." I took my tone down a bit, suddenly feeling guilty for what Grant had done to her—even if he did believe she was unfaithful. "I *am* sorry you're hurt."

"You love him, huh? Well, he loves me, and time will tell."

"Can time tell you to please get your disillusioned ass away from me! Seriously, we're old enough to know better. I don't fight, and I certainly don't fight over men."

"Men, huh?" she said as she tilted her head mockingly. "How many *are* you dating, Rose? Maybe I should let Grant know."

"Do whatever you want. *Talk* to whomever you want, but *please* get help somewhere," I said, looking for the closest escape route.

"I won't do that." I saw her lip quiver and her eyes fill with tears. "Look, I'm sorry for what I did to your arm. I just...miss him. I thought things were good." Her tears flowed freely, and it was then that I let my compassion take hold. I knew I would be devastated to lose him and hoped my fate would never be similar to hers.

"Can I ask you a question, Rebecca?"

"Why not?" she scoffed, eyeing me.

"Was he wildly romantic with you? Did he declare his love quickly and say...things, you know, to make you fall for him?"

"Wildly romantic? Grant? Ha! Grant doesn't have a romantic bone in his body. Who are you dating? He's a realist like me." My heart soared as she answered me, and I hastily changed my story to spare her.

"I didn't mean to imply he was romantic with me. I'm just curious."

She narrowed her eyes at me. This lady was no dummy. "I can't handle this. I really hate you. Fuck you both."

"Have a good lunch," I called after her. Poor guy, six months of that crap!

I pulled out my phone to let him know he had escaped a life of turmoil when I saw he was already calling. "Did you really go out with that unhinged thing for six months!?"

"She's a bit shallow, I know, but she has a decent heart. You just have to dig deep."

"I would have to dig forever. I can't believe you dated that *thing*."

"What happened?" I could hear his concern and smiled.

"Nothing I couldn't handle."

"I told you she was an in-between. I miss you."

"I don't blame you now for dropping her the way you did. I miss you, too. Are you on your way?" I felt a flutter of excitement race through me. He was what I looked so desperately forward to after a week with Dr. McGuire.

"No, I can't come. That's why I'm calling."

"Damn, I had dinner and everything...Oh, Grant, is it your dad? How is he?"

"It's pretty bad." The sadness in his voice let me know it was worse than usual.

"Oh, I'm so sorry."

"I don't know how long he has, Rose. I'm afraid I won't be back, you know...until after it happens."

"Oh, no, Grant, I miss you, but I understand. Look, I have some time off starting tomorrow. Can I come to you?"

"You'd do that?" His voice was shaky, and I could tell he was at his wit's end.

"Yes, of course. You're my future husband, right?" I teased.

"I sure am, baby. I need you so much."

"I'll leave tonight. Text me the address, okay?"

"I will. I can't wait to see you."

"Me too."

I loved him. I knew it. I had known it since our first date. It wasn't something that crept up on me. I knew, and the logical side of me fought it with everything I had until the romantic swooped in and pushed me over the cliff I had been teetering on. Grant never pushed me as hard after our day at the pond. He really never had to. It had been the most romantic month of my life. I accepted all he gave me with open arms. Loving him back was the easiest thing I'd ever done. Hearing Rebecca's words confirmed everything I thought about Grant after that day at the pond. This wasn't typical of him, not at all. I saw it in our time together after that fateful day. He had a good head on his shoulders, he often thought before he spoke, and was always the doting boyfriend. He worked hard and appeared smart with his money. He bought his land in his late teens and had just paid it off last month.

He kept his promise not to interrupt my schoolwork, often sitting on the couch with my feet on his lap while I had my face buried in books for hours. He never asked me for what I couldn't give and did his best to take care of me. I would see the look wash over him when he kissed or touched me, and I knew this was what love could really do. I believed that Grant was a realist because I was too—until we fell in love so quickly that it shook our belief systems to the core.

We spent a lot of our free days at his land, walking and talking about the future and getting naked underneath our tree, dreaming of the home he wanted to build. I would even entertain his idea that I would be a part of it all because I desperately wanted to be. For the first time in my life, I was letting the romantic reign, and it felt incredible. I was lost in love, and I didn't give a damn how hard I'd fallen back into reality the last time. My ex, David, had broken a piece of my heart but had never touched my soul. Grant moved me in a way that he had taken complete care of both. My heart was heavy with love—my soul was filled with contentment.

Sudden, maybe, but in my mind, the words were repetitive: *Just in time. Just in time.*

chapter
five

Rose

AS I BEGAN THE DRIVE, I WAS EXCITED TO SEE THE OTHER parts of Grant's life, yet I was saddened that I was about to meet his dad for the first and last time. He had been resisting his pain meds recently, and for Grant, it was agonizing. He would often scream out as Grant and I spoke on the phone. He had gotten a second wind in the last few days and was talking normally—which excited Grant—but I felt the dread in me as his excitement on the phone crossed the line. A second wind was often a sign that the end was near. I had spent hours and hours on the phone in the last month with the specialists, only to realize it was the worst-case scenario and there was nothing that could be done.

I drove through the night, thinking about the last time I saw Grant. He'd patiently waited all day as I performed a carefully constructed surgery on an orange on my kitchen counter.

I kept my headphones on as I cut into and stitched orange after orange, perfecting my technique. Vintage rap mix blaring, I got lost in my task, which apparently had lasted a lot longer than I thought. I could feel the soreness of being on my feet start to creep in but resisted. I needed to build my stamina. I was working on my last orange when my headphones were plucked out of my ears. I looked up to see Grant with the cord in his hand, "All I Need" by Method Man, resounding through the kitchen.

I gave Grant a smile. "Yes, dear?"

"I've been here for nine hours."

"Shit, really?"

"Yes, and I'm not mad. My dick is furious, but I'm not mad."

I laughed as I began to sway my hips to the music. "Good to know, and I'm so sorry," I said, snapping off my gloves. "I didn't mean to take that long."

"I told you I would be cool about it, and I will," he said, leaning in to give me a slow kiss. "But I'm starving and feeling slightly neglected and... I kind of like this song."

I looked at him curiously as he pulled me to him and cradled my body, and began to move. But not the way I expected him to. He was slow dancing with me to rap music.

"Grant, you do know this song is more upbeat, right?"

He ignored me as he moved his feet back and forth, dancing with me slowly until the song ended.

I took the exit for the highway that would lead me to him with only one thought on my mind—*he's perfect. Perfect.*

❧

I arrived early morning to a completely destroyed version of the man I'd been envisioning all night. I hadn't realized the toll his dad's impending death had taken on him. He greeted me at my truck door and wrapped his arms around me. I knew then that coming here was one of the best decisions I'd ever made. He hadn't asked, but I felt his need for me.

"Grant, it's time you let someone help you with this. It's

too much to shoulder alone." He pulled away, and I could see the dark circles underneath his eyes.

"The hospice nurse helps. I'm...I'm just...I don't know what I am, but I can't tell you how much this means to me. It means everything to me that you're here."

"I'm so sorry. I called everyone I knew. No one could draw a different conclusion," I said, feeling as if I had failed him.

"I know you did everything you could." He kissed my lips tenderly and, as an afterthought, added, "Do you think I expected you to save him?"

"I just really wanted to, I guess."

"And I love you more for it," he said, finally breaking our hug and grabbing my bag from my SUV. Grant hadn't said the words to me, and I was slightly stunned at his admission. I figured he would in his own time and that right now, he wasn't exactly worried about how I would interpret them. Still, something inside my chest squeezed hard.

His dad's house was nestled in the Smokies and looked exactly like Grant had described. It was a small log cabin and had a ton of charm. I fell in love with it instantly.

"You're going to sell it?" I said quietly as we walked to the doorway.

"I want the home in Texas more. Besides, I think this will be too painful, you know...without him here."

"I understand. I'm sorry I said anything."

"Don't be. I love it, too. I'll miss it."

His eyelids were slipping shut, and he was way too pale. Once he set down my bags, I ordered him to bed. He refused until I joined him, and we had our arms wrapped around each other. Once settled, he quickly fell into a deep sleep, and I got to work inside the house, cleaning, cooking, and preparing freezer meals for him to heat up.

I waited until his dad was awake to greet him. When I walked in, I immediately noticed he was a deep shade of yellow. His room was small compared to his large oak bed, and I scanned the machine next to it, assessing his vitals. My heart dropped when I took in his features. Grant was a carbon copy of his dad, who was currently gasping for air and moaning in pain. I stamped down my tears but had a horrible time with my quivering lip. It took all my strength to smile at him with my heart sinking in my chest. As a doctor, I'd seen cases like this without faltering. As someone that loved Grant, it was too much to bear.

"You must be Rose. Ah, honey, you're a dream to look at."

"I am, sir. Nice to meet you."

"Call me Davis."

"I will, Davis, thank you. How are you feeling?" I asked as I approached his bed with the confidence of the doctor I was training to be.

"Like I'm dying." His smile was supposed to comfort me, so I returned it the best I could.

"Well, let's at least take advantage of the good drugs. I'll administer this to you when the nurse comes back in."

"I want to be awake for this," he said adamantly.

"Davis." I started trying to get my wording right. "Grant told me you've been refusing the meds. I know you love your son, but please know he is losing his mind over this. I'm asking you for him. Please just take a little of the medicine so he doesn't have to hear you scream out, and so you can be a little more comfortable. We can give you a light dose. Please don't let this hurt more than it has to."

He simply nodded, and I took a seat next to him. As soon as the nurse returned, she happily administered the medication and left us to talk.

"His momma was beautiful, too. Did a number on me, but I expected it when I married her. She was way too antsy, never liked it here."

"Grant told me she left when he was very young."

"She was a decent mother to him. She just beat me to the punch," he said, gasping as more pain hit him.

"Davis, if it hurts you to talk, then I'll let you rest." I didn't realize I was holding my breath until his pain passed, and I exhaled.

"Oh, honey, I've been dealing with this shit for years. I'm ready, you know. I think I've just been hanging on for my boy."

I sat for hours by his side, horrified for what Grant had to endure as his dad drifted in and out on the morphine—a lot of his words incoherent. When he was finally peacefully asleep, I went to check on Grant, who was still out. I walked onto the back porch and looked around. Even though dusk had set, I could see dozens of tall pines in the backyard surrounded by scattered plane parts. I walked down, looking around at the various pieces of metal, and stopped at the lone cockpit of a small plane. Aside from the pilot and copilot seat, there was only a foot of space before the plane ended. It was simply a small piece of the whole picture, and I found it almost comical. Why in the world would anyone have so many worthless pieces of planes in their backyard?

"Hi, baby." I jumped a little as Grant approached. "Sorry, it was either warn you I was coming and scare you a little or scare the shit out of you a lot."

I giggled as I grabbed the hand he offered. "What is with the graveyard?"

"We were going to build planes together. That was our dream," he said as he lifted me into the copilot seat. I looked around with unease as he took his seat on the other side and let out a deep breath.

"A family business and all that, but he started drinking after my mom left us. It took a few years for him to bottom out. One of us had to be a grown-up. I hated him for it. I really did. I lost so much respect for him. Now I feel guilty for the words I said. He was just drinking through the divorce. You know, my mom broke him," he said with contempt. "She did. She broke him. And even when he eased up on the bottle, I refused to listen to him. I wouldn't let him back in. I was thirteen and I'd decided he wasn't worth it. I left to live with my mom, and I think it broke him even more."

I stayed quiet as he told me about his regret. I was sure he knew he wasn't to blame for his dad's mistakes or the fact that he was a rebellious teenager.

"I think, in a way, we killed who he was." He exhaled harshly, and I couldn't take it anymore.

"Stop it. You can't do this. You can't go there. Whatever you did years ago pales in comparison to the last few years."

"You're right. I know you're right."

"Don't start piling on the guilt. I'm sure he had his own to contend with. In the end, you love each other. In the end, he knows and feels that love from you, though it was always there."

"I love you, do you know that?"

I nodded as the blow hit me—the good kind of blow—the one with a force so strong that it knocked the breath out of you and made you want to live in that moment forever. He leaned in to kiss me, and I melted into it. When he pulled away, he gave a chuckle.

"Where to, Doctor?"

"You pick. I don't care where we go."

"And why not?"

"Because I'll be with you." He stopped his fidgeting with the knobs and looked at me with reverence. "I'll take that compliment, baby."

"Good, I hoped you would."

"God, this is so much better with you here." I gave him a grin as the cabin got darker, the night sky coming out to play.

"Grant, I think I want to add pilot to my list of career goals," I said, looking around, slightly excited. "I can so do this."

He turned to grin at me as I grabbed the wheel and started screwing with some knobs, having absolutely no idea what their functions were.

"Well, first of all, you just dumped half of your fuel," he said with a chuckle.

"Shit."

"And you'll need at least sixty to seventy spare hours."

"Double shit," I said with a sigh.

"We will get you there. Fuck, I'll have to work overtime to keep you satisfied. A surgeon and a pilot...What's next... president?"

"Maybe," I countered with a snicker. "You think they'll mind if I use a rap song for my campaign?"

"You'd definitely be original."

I looked around, still screwing with the gadgets, and excited about the thought of tooling around in a plane with Grant.

And for a few moments, we dreamed of the day we would build a small airstrip on his land.

"We could fly to Mexico for the weekend," Grant murmured, toying with switches that would never work.

"Mmmm...margaritas and ocean waves." We sat with the wind howling at our backs for over an hour, both of us getting excited about the future, stealing glances at each other's happiness. It was absolutely perfect.

The first night we agreed to take shifts at his dad's bedside since the hospice nurse only stayed a certain number of hours per day. Grant refused to wake me up, and when I woke myself, I knew it was late. I scolded him as I led him back to bed. "You aren't doing him a damn bit of good looking like shit."

"Uh oh," he said sleepily, "bitchy in the morning, are we?" I smacked him hard on his perfect ass as he gave me a sleepy grin before face-planting on his bed.

chapter

six

Rose

THE NEXT DAY I COOKED A HUGE BREAKFAST AT LUNCHTIME, knowing Grant would wake any minute. When he joined me in the kitchen, he gave pause in the doorway. "So, you're going to be a rich surgeon/pilot, you have the legs and ass of a supermodel, and you cook? No wonder I'm your bitch."

I burst out laughing as he piled pancakes on his plate. "Good morning to you, too."

"God, I needed that sleep." He pulled me onto his lap and kissed me soundly. "You tired?"

"A little but not enough to pass out."

"Then let me feed you." And he did, taking a large chunk of fluffy pancake and gently putting it into my mouth. I moaned in appreciation as he licked a bit of syrup off my lip.

"So fucking sexy," he murmured.

"Your dad is in earshot!" I protested.

"He probably thinks you're sexy, too."

"I do," I heard in a weak voice that managed to carry across the house.

"Pipe down, you old perv. She's definitely too good for you."

I slapped Grant's hands away as he groped me as much as possible, then made my way to Davis.

"How are we doing in here?" I asked as I stared at his full plate of pancakes.

"I just can't do it," he wheezed at me. "Please don't tell him."

"I won't," I said as I tossed the contents into the trash can next to his bed and pulled the bag out, sealing it. "Our secret."

"Thank you, darlin'."

I walked out of the room as fast as my feet would take me because I knew what was coming, and I couldn't bear it.

Hours later, I was at Davis's bedside as Grant ran some much-needed errands. We'd been working on a game of checkers for the better part of an hour as Davis faded in and out, growing weaker by the second.

"You love him, don't you?" It was barely a whisper, and though it took me by surprise, I gave him an honest answer.

"Yes, I do. With every single inch of me, I do. I love him very much."

"That's good news," he said weakly, trying in vain to come up with the strength to speak. I adjusted his pillow behind him. "He told me he'd found the woman he'd been looking for. The only time he smiles lately is when we talk about you." His face creased deeply with his attempt at a smile, and for a brief moment, I saw a glimpse of Grant as an older man.

I took the seat next to him and leaned into his line of

vision. "I've found my forever guy in him. He's amazing and warm and funny and caring and means everything to me. You did a fantastic job with him. I'll take good care of him, I promise."

"You already do." I turned to see Grant in the doorway, eyes wide and filled with emotion. He cleared his throat, smiling at us both. "I see you two have become well acquainted."

"Sure have, she's kicking my ass on the board, but she's been sweet about it." He smiled at his son, and I saw a wave of pain hit him. I stuck the needle into his drip and waited for him to nod yes as I squeezed a small dose of morphine in. I quickly cornered his bed and sat with him, holding his hand until I saw a small sign of relief on his pained face. I watched him slip off to sleep and felt Grant's hands on my shoulder.

"You look just like him, Grant."

"I know."

"He's a handsome man."

"So am I." I grinned up at him and could see a smile on his lips that didn't quite reach his eyes. He pulled the covers up over his sleeping dad, and I saw his face crumble in recognition that it wouldn't be long. Even I could physically feel his dad slipping away. I stood up and turned to him, wrapping my arms around him, trying to soothe him with my words.

"You are so amazing, Grant. He's lucky to have you as a son. You have taken excellent care of him. There really is nothing more you can do. Please know he loves you, and he knows you love him. I can tell you're the light of his life."

He took my hand without replying and led me to the back porch, which had an incredible mountain view on a clear day like today. I turned my eyes towards Grant just as he buried his head in his hands for a moment and then looked up at me with hopeful eyes.

"Do you really love me, or were you just saying that, you know...to make him feel better?"

"Of course I love you, Grant. I'm *crazy* in love with you, can't you tell?"

His eyes were swimming as he gently took my mouth. I cried into his lips, my confession making me tear up. I pulled back and gave him my heart with my next confession.

"I love you, Grant. You really are all I've ever wanted. I will build the house with you, and I want it all. You made me want more—you *are* the more."

He pulled me to him tightly, his lips meshing with mine as he held them there for a sweet and blissful eternity. When he pulled away, his emotions were etched on every feature. "This whole time, I was worried you thought I was truly crazy, and for a heartbeat, I thought you were just as nuts for going along with it, but it's so real. I mean, I felt it, I wanted to believe it, but now that I know for sure . . ." He pulled back and showcased his dimple. "I won't ever fuck this up, Rose. I won't ever give you a reason to want to walk away. I'll love you the way you deserve to be loved, always. That's my promise."

"I know."

"Marry me," he whispered softly.

"Yes."

It was that simple and yet so wholly satisfying. I didn't need a quartet or diamond ring. I didn't want rehearsed words, and I knew his proposal wasn't premeditated. Like everything else with us, it was on our time and perfect. We both stood in shock as we gazed at each other and then burst out laughing as we embraced.

"Holy shit."

"We are crazy."

"But we're the good kind of crazy. The kind that makes normal couples seem boring. You won't regret this," he said before he kissed me so deeply, I melted into him, my body molding perfectly with his. When we broke again, we laughed hysterically, our intention in sync as he led the way back to his dad so we could give him the news. When Grant paused at the doorframe, I ran into his back with a thud.

"Dad? Dad!" Grant raced to his dad's side as I moved frantically to the other, pushing a large dose of morphine into the needle. He buried his face in his dad's chest, and I saw Davis gasp again. He reached for Grant's hand, and I saw my love completely crumble as he said his last words to his dad. "You were the best dad a guy could ask for. I love you, Dad. I love you. I will see you again." I administered the larger dose of morphine as he slipped away, thanking me with his eyes. Davis moved into half-sleep and then passed away peacefully. Grant cried like a man who had just lost everything. I stood behind him, sobbing quietly, and watched the man I love go through the most horrible loss of his life.

chapter
seven

Rose

WE STAYED WITH DAVIS UNTIL THE MEDICS ARRIVED. When they wheeled his dad away, I followed Grant into his bedroom. We lay side-by-side on his bed holding hands, him crying for his dad and me crying for them both. I woke up hours later, not realizing I had dozed off, only to find Grant wide awake, still lying with me. He pulled me tighter to him when he noticed me stir.

"I'm so glad you're here. God, I don't know what I would do if you weren't," he whispered, his voice shaking as he lay next to me, staring at the ceiling.

"You're only twenty-nine, Grant, and you lost them both, way too soon. I can't imagine how much it hurts. I love you. You will always have me. I swear on everything. You will always have me."

A minute later, he spoke up again. "I shouldn't have proposed like that."

"No way, you don't get a do-over. It was perfect. Leave it alone. I mean it, Grant. I don't need anything fancy."

"Will you at least let me put a ring on your finger?"

"Absolutely, but we don't have to worry about that right now."

"How did I get so lucky?" He stroked my cheek, wiping away tears I didn't know I was shedding.

I turned to him, saying my next words with absolute certainty. "It wasn't luck. It was lightning." I held him to me as he mourned his dad. We cried together until we found a more peaceful sleep.

$$\sim$$

Grant walked me through his childhood home, telling me everything. We spent our days packing his dad's house and loading my SUV and his truck with priceless possessions he didn't want in the estate sale.

We spread his ashes at a gorge they often visited together throughout Grant's life. It was a small ceremony, and only a few attended. Grant held it together until that night, and when he finally broke, I broke with him.

The night before the estate sale, I packed my car to return to school. I'd missed an additional few days for Grant. I made apology after apology, but Grant seemed to fully understand and had no reservations, sending me off with a kiss.

"I love you, Mrs. Foster."

"I love you."

You know what?" he said as I threw my purse in the passenger seat.

"What?"

"We haven't even consummated our engagement." He leaned in closer, stealing my lips, his tongue whispering through them.

"I don't think that's a real thing, Grant," I said with a chuckle. "Matter of fact, I think it's noted somewhere in the book of morals that we not consummate our engagement."

"Unless you have that page in your hand, I'm afraid I'm going to have to disagree by initiating the act."

I chuckled, seeing him smile for the first time in days. "You've been busy, Grant."

"No, babe." He grabbed my hand and shut my door, pulling me back into the house.

"Grant, I have to go. Really, I can't stay," I said halfheartedly, wanting him just as much.

"Rose, I have to be inside you...right now." He scooped me up in his arms and took me into his bedroom. He took my clothes off piece by piece and covered every inch of my body with his kisses.

"Grant," I moaned breathlessly, all too eager for him.

"I have to make you come, baby. I live for it. Is that wrong? I just want to make you come, call my name, shake while I'm inside you. I want to feel you hot and wet around me and erase the world. I'm so addicted to you—to this." He dipped his head down and then licked me until I came, sighing his name. He climbed on top of me, his eyes deep pools of blue, so full of emotion and love for me. The slow descent of his head and his deep kiss were my undoing. His mouth drew everything from mine as my chest pounded in anticipation of his touch. He entered me slowly, inch by sweet inch, and I watched him shudder in satisfaction. His strokes were long and filled me to the brink—not an inch of me missed. The movement of his hips fueled the slow haze we were both drawn under, and I clenched around him, completely gone. He stopped suddenly, still wracked with emotion, and pulled me close to him, burying his head in my chest. I turned him on his back and pulled myself on top of him.

"I will do whatever you want, Grant. What do you want?" I was utterly intoxicated by him and wanted to soothe his heartache.

"You, just you," he whispered over and over as he started moving again, pulling my hips down to meet his length. The world could set fire, and neither of us would care when we were connected like that. The intensity we felt, our hearts and minds totally in sync, the feeling was un-paralleled. I called out, shuddering against him as he took his time filling me up, leaving me full, gasping, and comple-menting my name with his hoarse voice.

Once sated and dressed, he walked me back to my car and held me to him tightly. It had been an emotional couple of days, and I felt the urge to reassure him one more time.

"Whatever you want. I'm yours, Grant, always. I love you," I whispered to him before I slipped into my SUV. I dared not look back in the rearview, fearing I might fall apart. I'd left him alone to deal with his dad's estate, but a part of me knew it would only get him back to me sooner.

Grant

God gave us all the gift of intuition. If you aren't careful, it's easy to miss or ignore. I've always been really careful to listen to my gut. Like the time Tommy Andrews threw that curve ball, and I was sure of it and cracked that bas-tard out of the park. Or the time I avoided that bear trap on my first hunting trip with my dad. I didn't have to see it to know it was there. Then there was the time I was a couple of hundred dollars short of having enough money for my dad's meds and bought my first scratch-off ticket. Sometimes the gut knows before the mind has a chance to catch up. Tonight, I spent a fair amount of time thanking my intuition.

She was my match, my heart, my soul, my future, and not just because she was beautiful, and not because she was smart or funny and she got my jokes. It wasn't because of the incredible sex we had either or the way she looked at me, even though all these things contributed. It was the way I felt when I was with her. She had this effect on me like no one else ever had. I could climb and move mountains. I was stronger, braver, and I felt more like me, the me I was before the world's shit beat me down. I'd gladly take the scars I'd been given just to be able to appreciate the gift of knowing myself again through her. She did that for me.

She floats right in front of me now. She floats.

She floated around our engagement party, a woman with the same conviction that we're both part of a bigger picture, a picture we're about to paint together. I saw the love in her eyes for those around her and for me. I was sure I couldn't feel more full, happy, content, whatever you wanted to call it. It weakened me and made me stronger at the same time.

I looked around at the people admiring our connection, clinking glasses in celebration of us. I could feel their excitement for her, for me, for who we were together. They knew it, too.

"What are you doing?" she asked as I pulled out my hunting knife.

"Marking our tree, babe," I said as I dug my blade into the rough bark and cleared the way for our initials. We'd opted to come to the land at sunset after our engagement party rather than return to her apartment. It was our place, and I knew when Rose suggested it that she wanted to be here as much as I did.

"I don't have a suture kit out here," she said in warning.

"You aren't the only Foster good with a knife," I mused as she sat beneath me and inched away from the falling bark. I looked down at her reaction and saw her smile at the thought of her new last name.

"There's something about this place," she said in a whisper. "I can't explain it."

I smiled as I began to carve on the freshly uncovered wood. "You don't have to."

"It's like...it's exactly what I wanted. I just didn't know it." My grin spread as I pressed my knife in deeper with each word she spoke.

"I love when your dimple pops out. It's only when you smile like that."

"Hush, woman, I'm trying to do a manly thing here," I scolded as I glanced down at her. She sat in the grass, not giving a damn about ruining what I was sure was an expensive dress. She looked at the pond behind me in a slight daze.

"So peaceful, it's like a dream."

"I think I dreamed you into my life," I said, staring down at her perfect features. I was sure I'd never seen anything more beautiful as the fading sun glinted off her hair, making it a fiery red. She looked up at me with stunned amazement as I sheathed my knife and threw it to the ground, lifting her to see my handiwork. Wrapping my arms around her waist, I pulled her to me and whispered in her ear. "You cold?"

"No."

I kissed her neck and felt her shiver, knowing the cause was me.

"Your parents are amazing."

"Yeah, they are," she agreed, offering more of her neck, which I accepted.

"I didn't have to look hard to see what you were talking about. What they have is rare." I felt her smile and grip me tighter to her.

"Want to go?"

"Not really," she said, turning around in my arms to hold my face. I towered over her, but she'd never seemed intimidated by my size—even in the early days when I'd freaked her out. I think she secretly loved it, though she'd never said it.

In that minute, she looked at me and everything around us lit up in a gold and purple haze. I leaned in and kissed her deeply. She sighed into my mouth as I crushed my lips to hers, hungry yet gentle. I could see the intent in her eyes as we broke apart. She was hungry, too, but I played dumb.

"Want to go sew together some oranges?"

"No," she said with a furrowed brow.

"How about flashcards?" I said, turning from her to grab the champagne bottle we'd emptied.

"No," she said, giving me an odd look out of the corner of her eye.

"All right then. We can go through the medical journal—"

"What are you doin'?" she asked with a bit of bite to her voice. "I don't need to study today. Today is about us."

"I get that. But, baby, we spent a whole day celebrating, and you splitting and sewing up oranges is about us."

"I don't see you running off to work on a plane," she scoffed as I packed up the truck.

"Because I've been doing it my whole life, and when I see you practicing with your surgical kit, I can tell it makes you happy. I mean, we can bullshit around half the night, and you'll still end up sneaking out of bed to do a few, or you can just admit to me now that you want to go home and practice."

"I do not sneak out of bed," she said. "And it's not that interesting."

"It is to you," I said, crossing my arms as I closed the tailgate. She eyed me, unsure how to react. It was my chance to show her that in my heart of hearts, I knew I would have to share her with the world. She wasn't only a gift to me. She would be to other people, too. I took a step forward and lifted the cover off the cardboard box I'd stuck there this morning.

She looked at the huge pile of oranges, then up at me with a smile so beautiful it took my breath away. "I think I wished you into my life, too." She chuckled as she picked up and tossed around her newest cadavers. Worry covered her brow as she looked back at me for reassurance. "You know I love you, right? I mean, you know how important you are to me, right? And that spending time with you is just...it means everything."

I just nodded at her with a grin.

She shook her head, still a bit stunned, and then looked at me slyly. "How did you know?"

"Call it intuition."

chapter
eight

Rose

"**C**OME ON, WOMAN. I DON'T HAVE ALL DAMN DAY!"
"Seriously, you're acting like a total diva,"
I huffed, pushing my fingers through the lace
sleeves. "I mean, isn't that my job? I'm the one who is stuck
in here trying on tutus. Who thought of lace, anyway? This
is not cool."

"I did because you are the only woman past the eighties
who can pull it off!" The curtain moved, and Dallas's annoyed
expression turned soft. "God, I'm good."

"Seriously?" I asked, not having bothered to look in the
mirror.

"It was made for you. Turn around."

"No, tell me why you're so pissy. Aren't I the one that
should be downing champagne?" I took the tilted glass from
her and greedily drank the rest.

"Turn around," she said testily.

"No, you're ruining my day," I said, not giving a shit about
the fact I was trying on wedding dresses. Truthfully, I'd been
dreading it. I just never saw myself as a delicate bride. If I had a
real choice in the matter, I'd probably wear scrubs and Chucks

and walk down the aisle to old-school Eminem. Grant had insisted we do it a bit more traditional, and I'd reluctantly agreed.

"Sorry," she said with a sigh, her green eyes getting larger as she realized her behavior on what was supposed to be an important day for me. "God, I'm so sorry!" I saw emotion pass over her and guided her to the Victorian-style, plush green couch in the middle of the fitting room. It was the only thing in the room that wasn't white. Avoiding the vast row of mirrors, I turned to my sister with determination.

"Spill it," I said evenly.

"I finally broke up with Josh, and I feel so guilty. I was so wrong. What I did to him was wrong."

"So, your ex came back, and you didn't drop your boyfriend and go running back to Dean. It didn't take you another year to realize you didn't love him enough. It took you a month. Aside from the guilt, aren't you happy about Dean?"

"No, I don't want him, either."

"Liar. Wake up, stupid. Everyone at my engagement party knew you showed up with the wrong dude."

"Nice, Rose," she said, lifting a freshly filled glass of champagne to her mouth.

"I'm being nice. That's the nice way of putting it." I leaned into her. "I love you, but you've got a decision to make—shit or get off the pot with Dean. Seriously, the man is practically carrying his balls around in his hand."

Dallas spit out her champagne as she turned to me and began wiping furiously at the drops that didn't land on my dress.

"Stop it, it's fine," I said, pushing away her hands and stilling them. "You love that man." She averted her eyes, and I knew the subject was dropped before she spoke.

"Okay, no more talk about men. I'm totally done with them for the moment." Dallas's eyes softened even more as she studied me. "Rose, give me five minutes with what's inside my purse, okay? Just five minutes."

"Fine," I said, moving to sit back on the couch as she stopped me and turned me towards her.

"Still a tomboy in every way," she toyed as she pulled out her makeup bag.

"I just don't know why all this is even necessary. It does nothing but make us look like liars, you know. He'll know this isn't what I look like," I said, spitting out a fiber of powder brush caught on my lip.

"I believe the idea is to enhance," Dallas said, her eyes narrowing as she concentrated.

"It's not like I don't wear makeup. You aren't dressing a Neanderthal, woman!" I said defensively. But I was sensitive and uncomfortable with all of this, and Dallas knew it.

"Oh, so sensitive," Dallas teased as I resisted the urge to throttle her. "And lip gloss or Chapstick is not considered makeup. Hold still, or I'll do thicker eyeliner."

"The hell you will," I said as the sales clerk came in with shoes to match my dress, leaving bobby pins on the table beside Dallas, who gave her a thankful wink. Dallas layered my face in what felt like an exaggerated amount of cosmetics and had just fastened in the very last bobby pin available to my head as Jennifer burst through the boutique door.

"Sorry I'm late. Alex wouldn't let me leave until he got on the plane. You know he—"

I stood, nervously looking between the both of them as Jen's mouth dropped open in shock and instant tears fell silently down her cheeks. "Shit," she muttered as she took a step toward me.

"Shit," Dallas repeated as tears of her own fell rapidly from her eyes.

I reeled on my sister. "Dallas, you don't cry!"

"I know," she said, a small laugh-filled sob escaping as she nodded at Jen. I could practically see the mental fist bump between them. "You either," I scolded Jen as she rolled her eyes and wiped underneath them with her fingers.

I blew out a breath of frustration, turned to look at my reflection in the wall of mirrors, and froze.

"Shit," I muttered as a slow, pride-filled smile spread across my face, and a tear formed in the corner of my eye before it slid down my cheek.

Grant
Christmas Eve

"Foster, you're outta here. I can't afford any more overtime. Don't you have a bride to get to?"

Bride.

I smiled though I knew he couldn't see me. The smile wasn't for him, anyway. I couldn't wait for the moment it became the truth—just like I couldn't wait to kiss her for the first time that day under the tree. I admit I rushed it and chuckled when I thought back to how big her eyes got when I leaned in and pressed my lips to hers. Any trace of humor from her saucer-sized eyes that tempted me to laugh disappeared the second we connected. And that surprised moan in the back of her throat was all it took. I still couldn't believe all of the roads that interconnected perfectly to lead me to her. Even my parent's divorce, though as hard as that was for us all, had brought me to Texas, to her. I was sure—if I tried really hard—I could credit everything to fate or divine circumstance lending a hand. It was the new optimist in me, I guessed.

I loosened my grip on the wrench and watched it fall to my toolbox as I addressed the asshole ruining my thoughts of Rose.

"I just need five more minutes. I'm waiting on one last part, and she's good to go." I smack the side of the aluminum, two-seater duster I'd been repairing all day. But in truth, I was already done and was waiting for a delivery that didn't have a damn thing to do with the plane. Relief washed over me as the UPS truck pulled into the huge garage filled with needy aircraft. I was surprised the truck had actually made it this late on Christmas Eve. I approached the driver before anyone could and signed for the package. It was, after all, for me. I'd had it delivered here instead of Rose's apartment to make sure she had no way of seeing it until I was ready to give it to her.

I opened it, fiddled with the rubber and metal, and with a satisfied smile, left it in the box.

"That it, Foster?" my supervisor Troy asked, eyeing the box with suspicion.

"Yep," I declared, not giving him anything else.

"Five minutes," he said as he walked past me, turning off half of the lights.

"Asshole," I muttered under my breath as I made my way toward the plane and locked and tightened anything I might have missed. I checked and rechecked my work, hearing my dad's stern voice as I wrapped up.

"Everything is put in its place for a reason. You hear me, son?"

"Yes, Daddy," I said as I tightened the bolt as much as I could.

"Okay, now check your work."

"Yes, sir. Daddy, why—"

"Enough with the whys for one day, son." He smiled down at me. You aren't looking at the big picture. One day, it's all going to click into place for you, and you'll know the why of everything."

"Foster, if I didn't know better, I would say you were dragging ass just to piss me off!"

Even my moody boss couldn't put a damper on this night—no one could. I'd finally found her, the woman who both terrified me in my feelings for her and made me a better man. Though she'd tried to make it complicated, it really was so simple.

The truth was, I'd acted like a goddamn maniac since the minute I saw her and didn't stop until she agreed to become Mrs. Maniac. Closing my eyes, I damn near moaned at thoughts of what I would do to her tonight and tomorrow night, but only after I gave her what was in this box. In one week, every damned dream I had was coming to life. Well, in truth, everything I'd worked for, the land, getting back to Texas, none of it had made real sense until I figured out that I wasn't doing it for me. My dad was right—it had all clicked into place, both in the mechanics and in my life.

Everything and every experience I'd ever had were leading me to this point. I had planted the seed of a future for myself a long time ago without ever really seeing the bigger picture. To my credit, I did have a glimpse of what I wanted, but it wasn't until I met Rose that the future became paved, solid, and far more beautiful.

Rose made me laugh like no other woman had ever managed and had the ability to bring me to my knees with one look.

These are the things I'd looked for and failed to find in other women. No one had ever even come close. She was never really a mystery to me, but I damn sure stayed intrigued every time she opened her mouth. She was brilliant without trying to be and had a nasty bite that I loved to temper when I pissed her off. I loved her passion for her work but knew she would drop her scalpel in a heartbeat for anyone important in her life if they needed her—for her family, for me.

Last night as we lay tangled up in each other's arms, I asked her how she felt about marrying a roughneck. It was a bit of an insecure moment for me, I admit, but leave it to my 'tell it like it is' fiancée to give me the perfect reply. She simply looked up at me and said she would choose to marry a man who earned everything he had rather than one who had shit handed to him because she knew he'd worked just as hard as she had. And in her eyes, it made us equals. Then she proceeded to curse me out for thinking she was any better than me. And then I pinned her beneath me and kissed her naturally red lips breathless.

She was made for me, and me for her. I did the right thing by leaping out of that truck after her—even if I did make a damn fool of myself. Maybe I fell in love with the idea of her first. Either way, I'd make no apologies now for any of it because she'd captured me now, heart and soul, on every level. It was my job to protect her, but if I were being honest, I felt the safest I'd ever had in her love for me.

My idea turned into my everything, and I wouldn't change a fucking second.

Yes, she was made for me—and she told me so. I'd had the proof in my wallet for the last four months—but never showed it to her.

She believed in signs, and even though she'd already agreed to be mine, I knew this would solidify what we already knew. I took the piece of paper out of my pocket. The same piece of paper that had me chasing after her with an answer.

She'd been practicing her signature. I found it adorable, but what got me was the bottom of the page...

I pulled the engraved stethoscope from the box again and knew I'd answered the questions she had written on that piece of paper. Holding the circular end of it, I rubbed my thumb over the etched words, reveling in the answer.

Dr. Foster

"Foster!"

"All right, you greedy bastard, keep your overtime!" I look over at Troy, who gives me a shit-eating grin with an undertone of serious distaste.

"Done, and don't think I won't dock your pay for every minute you've kept me waiting."

"Dock me," I snapped, closing my toolbox while whistling

Dixie. I brushed past Troy with a "Merry Christmas, Scrooge. I sure hope there are no Tiny Tim's in your neighborhood, for they will surely starve."

"I have a damned Barbie house to put together and two bikes," he groaned as he slid the hangar door shut, then locked it.

I grinned at his back, hoping for the same circumstances to bitch about someday. I couldn't wait to see whose genes won out, Rose's or my own. If I had to guess, I was pretty sure the 5' 6", red-haired goddess I was about to marry would win that war. I was also sure I wouldn't give up after the first battle.

I got into my truck and blew hot air into my hands, rubbing them together while it warmed up. I couldn't help my excitement as I pulled out the stethoscope again and tested it on my own heart. I could only hope she would understand the significance of the note.

Of course she would. She'd been just as surprised by the freight train that ran us both over as I was, even if that freight train was me.

A year ago—on this very night—I'd fisted a bottle of Jack Daniels while my dad slept uncomfortably, crying out in pain every so often. It was a shitty existence to live for someone you knew was about to die and not have a damn thing to look forward to. I'd drowned my sorrows in a bottle, making my new year's resolutions early. I'd decided I would, by the same time next year, have something to look forward to.

And God, wasn't she something.

I pulled out my phone, looking for any word from her as I glanced at my dash clock.

Rose: Hurry up, roughneck. I love you.

Pulling out a small gift bag and tissue paper I had ready, I carefully wrapped the stethoscope and note inside it—along with a note of my own—and then tucked the bag under the passenger seat where it would stay hidden until we got back from her parents on Christmas Day. I got her a slew of shitty gifts just to deter her from this one, and I couldn't wait to see her face when she opened the first shit gift tonight—a duck caller from the online Duck Dynasty store. I would tell her it was for our new pets. I burst out laughing as I imagined her confused face when she opened it. I had to get my laughter out now before I was forced to hold back in her presence. If she seemed too disappointed, I'd race out to this truck and make it up to her.

Anything for her, always for her...my something to look forward to.

chapter
nine

Rose

"MERRY CHRISTMAS, JENNIFER!"
I threw the bags filled with presents inside our apartment, then started wrapping as fast as I could. Grant was due back from work any minute, and I didn't want him to see what I'd gotten him. We had set a date to marry on New Year's Eve, and our apartment was flooded with packed boxes. Jennifer was moving to California after our graduation ceremony next month, but I couldn't justify moving my husband in with us. We had found a rental home close to ground zero of our ranch home. The foundation had already been poured, and most of the framing was done. I was beside myself with my excitement. Our wedding would be a small intimate ceremony at my parent's house.

I'd never wanted a huge wedding, and Grant seemed to only want the title of husband. I'd spent a majority of the day finalizing all the details with my mom—who was just as excited—and spent way too much money on pre-wedding pampering. I was anxious to share the details with Grant but more so about the bow-covered negligee I had purchased today. Being with Grant had released the vixen in me. Not only that, the woman I'd sworn I'd be someday. I'd never felt more feminine, more beautiful, or more cherished. I couldn't wait to wear the dress I'd dreaded picking out for him.

I'd also gotten a ton of food and booze for a private little Christmas Eve feast. Not only did I have a wedding to look forward to, but I'd also earned the interview with Dr. McGuire.

"Merry Christmas, you happy bitch," Jennifer said, rolling her eyes when I cued up the Christmas tunes.

"I know. It's totally annoying, isn't it?" I said, taping my first box and throwing it to the side to start the next.

"Wow, am I glad I let that guy in!" she noted as I sang along to the Drifters' "White Christmas".

"I know. I am, too. That's why I got you this." I threw the gift at her, smacking her in the head on accident and wincing as she gave me the evil eye.

"Sorry!"

She hastily opened the tiny box and smiled.

"You really are doing this?" She took the bridesmaid neck-lace from the box and put it around her neck.

"Four months is crazy, I know, but I can't live without him."

"He is your match, Rose. I've been your best friend for years, and you've never been this happy, even with what's his face."

"Don't even say it," I warned. "That wasn't even love."

My phone rang, and I saw the picture of Grant and me in front of our tree the day the foundation was poured.

"Hi, my love. Are you on your way?"

"Yes, and I'm about to lose it thinking about what you did to me last night." I giggled like an idiot as Jennifer rolled her eyes and headed to the kitchen, mumbling about something to do with her being excited about privacy. I ignored her to tell my fiancé about the night I had planned for us.

"I got eggnog, champagne, and shrimp. Enough for us both to eat."

"A boat full?" he teased.

"Shut up and hurry up. I love you."

"I love you, baby. See you in a minute."

"One week left, Mr. Foster. You sure you don't want to back out?"

"One week and forever, baby. I promise."

I waited for Grant for two hours in my negligee-clad body, surrounded by candles burning, before the sinking feeling took over. I started calling hospitals, starting with the ones I knew were on his route. It only took two calls to find him.

The doctor in me listened to Grant's attending objectively. He was pronounced dead at the scene. I knew that though the doctor didn't say it. I was certain by the extent of his injuries that he hadn't felt much or anything at all. He was on his way to me, and the idea that he might not make it there had probably never crossed his mind. He'd had no time to process. It was too sudden. I knew that. And it was the only thing holding me together as Jennifer sobbed by my side.

It had been a freak accident.

That was what they said to me.

A freak accident had stolen my whole life from me.

I hoped I was pregnant.

That was my first clear thought, and I couldn't even justify how unreasonable it was. I sat on the toilet in my parents' bathroom hours after losing Grant, hoping we had somehow fucked up our plans to wait.

I wanted a piece of him to live and grow inside me, a piece of us. I prayed then for every possible imaginable failure in birth control. Scenarios of being a mom raced through my mind as I wondered what he or she would look like. I hoped it was a boy and had Grant's beautiful locks. I would never cut his hair. He would be a replica of his dad. I would decorate his room in planes, and we would talk about him every day. We would live in our ranch home, and he would grow up tall and strong like his dad, with a heart just as golden. It was the first time I'd actually imagined a child with him. I'd been so sure I had time to daydream about that once we were married and I'd met my career goals.

We would have kids as soon as I finished my surgical program. We'd decided that together. Well, actually, Grant had wanted them sooner. We'd even fought about it once, but he'd relented so easily when I insisted we wait a little longer. *Everything* we'd decided revolved around *my* life's plans. Grant just wanted to give me everything I wanted—now *all* I wanted was him and a different reality.

For the first time in my life, I no longer wanted to be a surgeon because being a surgeon was selfish.

I stared at the urine-covered stick hiding in my parents' bathroom and prayed like I'd never prayed in my life for that word to appear...and it did with a big fat fucking NOT in front of it. I grabbed a hand towel and gripped it between my teeth, and bit down, screaming in agony as if being pregnant with his child would save me in any way from the hurt that was stretching my chest so painfully. And suddenly, breathing was a chore.

Breathing is an involuntary movement. You learn that in

basic science in grade school. I say that fact turned false for me the minute I lost him. I was no longer breathing without doing it for myself. I had no help. It was up to me.

As I threw the useless stick of devastation away, I had a new and sudden list of the things I didn't care about. I didn't care that I was still young and had a promising career ahead of me. I no longer cared that I had a long list of people that loved me and would still be there for me through thick or thin. I no longer cared for the interview I'd worked my whole life for. I no longer cared about any of it. None of it brought me any happiness. None of it could replace or even come close to what I'd just lost.

"If you would have only left *one* minute sooner," I whispered to him. "Why couldn't you have just left sooner?"

Timing, that's the last thing I had thought about before I stood, body and mind giving out in perfect unison.

I regained consciousness on the floor sometime later as my dad knocked softly on the door, my face planted on the carpet, and my body twisted unnaturally. I'd never fainted before and was still unsure of my faculties when he spoke.

"Rose, do you need anything?" I turned on my back to stare at the ceiling and cursed the carpeted bathroom for saving me. I wanted to feel physical pain in the worst way at that moment, to blanket the unbearable pain in my chest as the realization hit me again.

Grant's dead.

My throat was dry, and I could barely get the words out. "Daddy...I'm...okay...Daddy."

"Come out when you're ready." I sensed his hesitation at the door before he walked away and swallowed hard at his words because I knew I wouldn't ever be...ready. I didn't want to see my family stare at me for my reaction to what just happened and cater to my tears because they would be endless. I gasped as my mind came into focus, and his face flashed across it, along with his words after our first kiss.

"Did you feel that?"

Of course I had felt it. It was lightning. We were a sudden anomaly in a sea of lost people. We'd found it right then. The thing that everyone wants. The thing that everyone should experience in their lifetime. It was real. The romantic in me believed him in an instant. It was as if he'd awakened her with his conviction—and I'd initially ignored her.

Why couldn't I have acknowledged sooner that I was right there with him in every moment? Why did I have to try so hard to deny what was instantly between us? The recognition? The connection? I was such a bitch to him at first, so eager to prove him wrong. I lost a month of reveling in our love by denying it was possible. A month, a second, a minute, a breath, I had no idea how precious our time was.

He's gone.

No, he's *dead*. Gone would indicate that he would be back again one day. And that fact was the razor blade that cut endlessly through my aching soul again and again as I pulled in another breath and held it.

I felt a colossal lump in my throat as tears streamed down my face. Still staring at the ceiling, I ignored the sting on my cheeks. I had no will to move from that spot. I was comfortable and warm and had absolutely no intention of leaving. There was nothing outside that door that I wanted. Behind it represented the future, and I was more than happy to pretend it didn't exist.

I was a widow. God, I didn't even have time to earn that title. Oh, and God, where were you, and why didn't you save him?!

I gripped the carpet in my hands, pulling at it as the burn overtook me, and I lost myself again to my grief, my sobs uncontrollable. I didn't want to be there at my parent's house. I didn't want them to hear me cry. I felt like I needed to scream over and over, but I didn't because I knew what it would do to my parents—to my brother and sister. No, I couldn't even grieve the way my soul was begging me to.

Grief, what a shitty word for what this feels like. They should rename it.

Agony wasn't even a decent enough word.

Hell couldn't even touch this.

And still, the word death fits perfectly.

"You took me with you," I whispered to him again. "I can't do this, Grant. I can't."

As a child, I had conjured an amazing story in my mind. It was a story I could retell about a man that would move me like no other—a story about the way we met and how he had swept me off my feet. But, the ending to that fairytale was so far from reality. It involved years of a happy marriage and endless memories...not months. No one will want to hear our story now.

Grant and I fell in love in a lightning strike. It dissipated just as quickly as it struck—gone in a blink of an eye. Life had given us a great big period at the beginning of our sentence, and now I had a life sentence to serve without him.

No, no one will want to hear the end of our story. It will sadden them and make them come up with awkward words of half-assed condolence because they don't have any fucking idea how bad this feels. Or maybe they do and won't want to relive it when they look at me. Either way, it was too short. There isn't much to tell. But my heart and mind protested in that instant because I'd felt full with him. And as I lay on my parents' bathroom floor, my mind swirled as I gripped and clung to every memory that flashed past me, pulling it close to my aching chest.

"Please, stop beating," I begged my heart, then addressed my mind. "Shut it off. Please, just shut it off."

"Rose?"

It was Dallas. I turned my head to look at the door but remained silent. I was sure she'd heard me, and I was almost positive she'd been sitting outside the door the whole time.

"Rose, you've been in there for six hours. I swear to God, I want to leave you alone, but I can't. I can't. Please open the door."

Ignoring her plea, I lifted my hands and stared at them. These hands would eventually be able to reattach pieces of human flesh in the intricate way of a skilled surgeon. They would repair damage to vital organs. They could eventually fix the heart so it beat rhythmically. That would be my gift. At one point, I thought it was the only one I would get. I was fine with it. My heart didn't know any differently. It needed no repair. I could laugh now at the pain I thought loving David caused. It was completely insignificant in that moment. I'd mourned nothing.

But this...this was what it was truly supposed to feel like, the finality, the loss of the most significant piece of yourself. *This* was what it meant to have your heart broken.

No, the damage to my heart was done by the second gift

I'd been given, and now, no matter how skilled my scalpel became or how sharp I remained in mind, I couldn't do a damn thing about the damage to my own heart. My hands were useless.

No, I was never leaving this room.

❧

"Mrs. Parker," I heard Dallas sob. I knew she was trying her best to make sure I didn't hear her hushed conversations, but I did. Thankfully, I was numb to them. "This is Dallas Whitaker... there's been an accident." Dallas's voice cracked as she tried her best to remain strong as she went through my guest list to inform each and every person that expected to attend our wedding in a few days that the groom had passed. And instead of a wedding, they would have to attend a funeral. I loved Dallas more in those moments because I could hear the heartbreak in her voice for Grant. She was feeling his loss deeply, not only because she loved him but because she loved me. It brought me a strange comfort to hear her strangled conversations. "Grant had passed and, of course, the wedding . . ." There was a pause as shock registered to the caller, followed by what I was sure was the inevitable plea to pass on condolences.

Another fucking stupid word.

"I will let her know," I heard Dallas pause, then plead with my mom in the kitchen, probably cupping her hand over the phone as Mrs. Parker wept. "Mom, I can't do this anymore." I heard my mom's voice immediately.

"I'm sorry, Mrs. Parker, Dallas is a bit upset. Yes, of course, I'll relay the message to Rose."

But my mom wouldn't relay anything because she knew

I didn't want to hear words of condolence. I pulled the quilt I'd been comforting myself with since I was a kid closer to my chest as I stared through the small crack in the closed blinds. The weather was dreary, and I was thankful. I didn't want to see the Texas sun. I didn't want to be reminded of its existence and how—for a brief moment—I had owned a piece of it.

⁓

The mind is a cruel thing. I was now a firm believer that it controls your heart. We're led to believe they're two separate but powerful adversaries battling it out for control, but I no longer see it as the case. Every waking moment of the past week, my thoughts had only led my heart to bleed. It had no say—it just kept obeying my relentless mind, the ache, the pull, the never-ending tear that ripped at me with every second of awareness that he was gone.

My weak heart never had a chance against my mind, which I decided loved Grant the most because it kept perfect memories.

I stood in my satin and lace wedding dress, on my eventless wedding day, staring at the pond where we fell in love. Every memory we had there, even our first fight, was perfect.

"*Will you stop already?*"

"*Never,*" Grant said with a slight grin.

"*You're impossible!*"

"*No, I'm right, and you know it. We'll never really be ready. No one ever is.*" He shrugged as he started to walk back to his truck, which angered me to no end.

"*Don't walk away from me! I'm still talking to you!*"

"*Can we talk on the way back? I have a long shift.*"

"No."

"Fine," I heard him grunt out as he turned to me, his hands behind him on the hood of his truck, his legs crossed at the ankle. He was irritated. It was the first time I'd seen him angry. I had to hide my smile because, even angry and frustrating as hell, he was the most lovable man in the world.

"When you asked me to marry you, I didn't hesitate. I didn't want to, but, Grant...I can't give a baby the attention it needs, not now."

"I know."

"So, if you know, why are you pressuring me?!"

He crossed his arms and looked at the pond behind me. "You wouldn't understand."

"Oh, well, there's communication," I snapped, walking towards him for an explanation.

"You have this great family."

I understood immediately. He wanted his own. "They're yours, too."

"I want our family. That's all I want. I can't stop this need in me, Rose, and as soon as I found you, it was all I could do to keep my mouth shut. I think my parents' deaths changed me. I think as soon as I saw how mortal we really are, I wanted life then and there. And I know it's unreasonable in a way, but here we are, a month away from marrying. Your career is set, and so is mine, and we're building this amazing house."

"What if I don't want to become a mom right now?"

Grant studied me briefly before scrubbing his face with his hand. "Fuck, I'm sorry." He walked over to his passenger door and opened it, then looked at me with pleading eyes. "I'm sorry. It's too much to ask. I just...fuck, I won't ask this of you, not now." I ignored the open *door as I approached and searched his eyes, seeing the same sadness in them as I did the minute his dad passed.*

"I want everything you want, Grant. If I didn't, I wouldn't have agreed to this life with you. But you have to stop this race. We have all the time in the world, and even if I were to get pregnant tomorrow, a baby couldn't replace what you've lost. You're grieving and think you need something to fill the void."

He nodded as a single tear fell down his cheek. I went to him, wrapping my small frame around him as much as I could as he gripped the back of my shirt with his fists, burying his head in my neck. I didn't have to tell him about the sudden panic racing through me that our fast love and shotgun wedding might have been a reaction to his dad's illness and death. I didn't want to believe it for one second. Still, it paralyzed me even as I was consoling him. It was a selfish thought, and I hated myself for it.

"I still feel the hole of his absence even when I'm with you, Rose. You aren't a cure for any of that. I know what you're thinking, and I want you to stop."

"Maybe we should wait—"

"If you finish that sentence, I won't forgive those words." He looked up at me then, so raw but so certain. I simply nodded as he leaned in. "This is not manufactured love." He turned and sat in the passenger seat, then pulled me to straddle his lap. We said nothing as we stared at each other for long minutes before his lips descended slowly onto mine. His kiss was deep, raw, and filled with emotion and love. Just as certain as he was, I leaned into him, his strong arms caressing me, his fingers running through my hair as he soothed me right back. When he pulled away, our argument was over. Not because either of us won but because we both wanted the same thing. We both knew that, eventually we would get it.

I would have everything I'd asked for, and he would have the family he'd always wanted.

I threw the last of the feed into the pond and watched the ducks eat their fill. Could they feel his absence, too? Did they know that he was gone?

Grant had faced mortality head-on, several times. He *knew*. I'd lost absolutely no one close to me in my life until him. Suddenly, the realization of why he'd wanted a family so much hit me harder. All he had was me...me and those damned ducks. Who else would miss him? Who else would know who he truly was?

It was up to me to remember him and me alone. His friends—though present at the funeral—were too few and too far removed from his life because of traveling to care for his dad. They didn't have memories of him now—they were ghosts of his former life, a life where he was carefree and not shouldering the responsibility of a dying parent.

If I forgot him, he would be forgotten.

I vowed then and there to never let that happen.

chapter
ten

I ENTERED MY PARENT'S HOUSE TO FIND THEM IN THEIR RECLINERS, locked in an obvious battle of wills. I stood in the entryway listening to their fight as I laughed to myself, peeking around the corner.

"Give me the damn remote."

"No!"

"I'm not watching this reality shit anymore, Seth. Give it to me."

"No."

"Seth, I'm going to kick your ass all over this house."

I had to cup my hand over my mouth to keep from bursting.

Only my mom.

"There are seven TVs in this house, Laura. Go find another one." I heard my dad sneeze and grab a tissue. I could only see the back of their heads in their separate recliners as they sat side-by-side, bitching over their shared coffee table.

"Seth, I am warning you, and you won't like me when I'm angry *and* sick."

"Nothing new. You're the biggest pain in the ass I've ever met. If you think I haven't seen you at your worst, you're nuts."

"That's it. Give me the remote!"

"No," my dad protested with a bark. "Laura, you're getting to be a mean old woman."

"Did you just call me old?" An eerie silence filled the room as my dad feared for his life.

"Here, take it." I saw the remote being lightly thrown into my mom's chair as my dad cowered in his.

Good move, Dad.

"You're still beautiful, baby."

"Save it, Seth. You are screwed for the day."

"Come on, baby, don't be mad."

"You are the one with brittle bones. Better take it easy before you break a hip."

"I'm sorry, baby."

"Forgiven, but we're still not watching this crap." I smiled as my parents coughed in unison, then took the step up leading into our living room.

"House call."

My mom's eyes brightened instantly as I came into view. "Oh, Rose, baby, how are you? You're all I think about." My mom's sick, nasally voice instantly tugged at my heart. She'd always been such a strong woman. Any sign of weakness usually got to me when it came to her. I kept my tears from coming and gave her the new usual, "I'm fine, Mom." She reached out to hug me, but I brushed past her with a soft kiss on her cheek.

"I'm fine, really." I saw her hesitate, then look at my dad, hurt on her face.

"Don't lie to me, Rose. I know how bad you're hurting," my mom said, sitting back in her recliner.

Fast-growing anger boiled inside of me. "Do you? It sure seems like you don't, Mom." I looked between her and my dad, then shook my head. I sat on the couch and apologized under my breath.

"Don't say you're sorry. You're right. I don't know. I don't have any idea. Talk to me, Rose," my mom said, begging me for anything. She had done nothing but reach out to me for weeks, and I'd shut her out. I could tell it was hurting her, but I couldn't share my pain with her. I stood up and popped the thermometer in between the two of them. The longer I was with them, the angrier I became. I resented their happiness. It was a grudge I had no right to hold, but still, it lingered.

"No temperature. Looks like a nasty cold. You need fluids and rest, and stop fighting over the remote." I saw them grin at each other, and I took a deep breath before rolling my eyes. My dad noticed.

"What is it, baby girl?" my dad asked, apprehension apparent in his tone. "You can tell us anything."

"Nothing, Daddy. I have to get back."

"Rose, talk to us, please. This is the first time we've seen you since the funeral. I've been to campus and your apartment four times. You won't return my calls. Don't shut us out like this," my mom pleaded.

"I don't want to talk."

"Rose, you went back to school, and we didn't think it was the best idea. At least pretend you still need a little parenting now and then to flatter us," my dad added.

"Grant's dead. What is there to say? I'm a twenty-five-year-old widow."

I saw my dad hang his head and carefully survey me again. "I love you, little woman. Don't forget that you'll always have us."

"And *you two* will always have *each other*." I heard the

venom in my voice and saw my mom flinch at my statement. It was wrong, I knew it was wrong, but it didn't make my need to flee any less strong.

"Rose, I don't care how mad you get or what you say, please, just let it out...just say it," my mom begged again.

"I'm fine, okay?! I'm working, I'm eating, and I'm even doing my fucking laundry. I'm fine."

I saw calm wash over my mom's face and paused my rant. "Hear that, Seth? She's fine. You know what? I feel fine, too. How about you, Seth? You feel fine?" She tossed the blanket off her legs and stood up, throwing her blanket in her chair.

"Mom, you really are sick. Sit down. You need to rest. I'll make you some soup."

I headed to the kitchen, my mom hot on my heels.

"No, I'm great. As a matter of fact, I think I'll go for a swim." I heard the sliding glass door open behind me as I reached the cabinet and chased her down when I saw her taking off her slippers.

"Mom, it's freezing! It's forty-five degrees out here!"

"I'm fine!" she mimicked, sounding eerily like me.

"Laura, what in the hell *are* you doing?" I heard my dad's voice boom behind me.

"Seth, why don't you join me?" She wiggled out of her robe and, without a moment's hesitation, dove head-first into what I was sure was ice-cold water.

"Damn it, Laura!" my dad yelled as he made his way over to her, as she emerged with a gasp.

"Oh, my God, Mom!" Following my dad, I shooed him away at his attempt to get to her first and pulled her out by the hands, feeling the freezing cold water hit my arms and shivering as she looked at my dad with an eyeful of 'Don't say a word.'

"You're going to get yourself killed, Mom! You could catch pneumonia!"

"I'm fine."

"Cut it out, Mom!" I pleaded as my dad did his best to stifle his anger. I ran to the living room, grabbed a blanket, and made it back to the kitchen, wrapping it around her as she walked inside.

"I get it, Mom. You're trying to prove a point. And you took it a little too far, might I add."

"I'm fine, Rose." She began to shake, and my dad tried to put his arms around her to get her warm.

"I'm fine!" She brushed him off, opened the freezer door, and stood there shivering.

"Damn it, Mom, I get it, okay? I won't say I'm fine again. I'm miserable."

She studied me with sharp eyes before bursting into tears. She shut the freezer door and approached me with a seriousness reserved for talks like this.

"You are my baby, Rose—*my* baby. When you hurt, *I* hurt, and that's the way this works. I was no more ready to jump in that pool than you were to dive right back into life. You need me, and I need you more because you're everything to me. If I can see your pain—even when it's at its worst—I can still see *you*, Rose. And if I can still see you, I can sleep at night. I'm selfish, I guess, but I need to be here for you through this. We both do."

I looked at the pain etched on my parents' faces and crumbled. "I won't hide it anymore, Mom." I buried my head in my hands and heard my voice whisper, "Why did this happen to me? To him?" I began to cry as my dad caught me in his arms. I heard my mom let out her own anguished sob as my dad pulled her into us. We stood huddled in the kitchen as my mom shivered and my dad soothed us both.

"I don't know why. I've been asking the same thing over and over. All I can tell you is that I'm with you. Through every minute of this, we are with you." I sniffed and nodded as I pulled away from them with a small smile.

"I know, and I love you both. I'm sorry I haven't been by. God, Mom, you are *crazy*! I would almost think you got your-self sick so I would come home."

I saw my dad smile and gave them both a look of shock. "You are kidding me!"

"Of course not. How is that even possible?" I saw my mom look at my dad, then give him an 'I told you so.'

"Laura, baby, go shower and change." My dad slapped my mom's butt, and I saw her give him a wary glance.

"I don't take orders, Seth."

"Pretty please, pain in the ass? You've been in that robe for two days."

"Fine." She scurried away, no longer hiding the fact that she was freezing to death, and I looked on after her with amuse-ment. My mom hung the moon as far as I was concerned, and my dad was my hero. I sighed as I looked at him while he watched my mom retreat with awe on his face.

"She's amazing, right?"

"I'm so jealous, Dad," I admitted as he turned to look at me, confused.

"Jealous?"

"Yeah, you two have had each other for almost thirty years, and I only got months."

"Is this why you stayed away?"

I sat down at the kitchen table and hung my head.

"Lightning struck with Grant, Dad. It's over for me. I can't even imagine loving anyone else, ever."

"It's too soon to say that, but I can tell you now, we aren't the type to give our hearts away to just anyone, Rose. We choose carefully, and then we're all in. Don't rush life. Let it happen. You can't rush your way through the grieving, and you sure as hell can't go on working yourself out of it. Take your time, sweetheart. Let it hurt, and let us hurt with you."

chapter
eleven

Eight Months Later

"SEVEN HOURS OF PERFECTION, ROSE. I'M TRULY IMPRESSED. I have to say, I have never sat back and watched any surgery without interrupting during the fifteen years I've headed this program.

"Thank you, Dr. McGuire," I said, snapping my gloves off and trashing my smock.

"I'm truly impressed. Get ready for greatness. I'm bumping you to the top of the list."

"No, sir, please don't do that. I wouldn't feel comfortable."

"This isn't about the comfort of your peers. This is about us honing your skills. They'll deal with it. It's a competitive field."

"I'm more than happy to assist, sir."

"This is not a discussion," he scolded as we walked down the corridor toward the nurses' station.

"Yes, sir."

I listened to the doctor dispense orders to two of the nurses about patient aftercare. He seemed puzzled that I was still standing next to him as he turned to look at me. "I want you to go home. I won't schedule your next surgery for a couple of days. Take some time, reflect, and recharge."

"Sir—"

"This is also not up for discussion, Rose."

"Yes, sir."

⁓

I drove straight to Grant's land for the first time since I graduated medical school. I'd come here right after losing myself in my memories, holding them closer than ever. It was a pivotal moment, and Grant wasn't there to celebrate with me. I was lost all over again.

It seemed the new owners hadn't done anything with it. I was still cursing myself for not moving on it faster when it went into probate. I was too lost in losing him that I couldn't think of anything else. And by the time I had, it was too late. Now, it just sat there untouched.

I had two days of nothing to do and couldn't figure out a way of passing the time other than to visit the place that I loved the most. I'd spent every waking moment either practicing surgical techniques or in surgery. Time off was a nuisance to me. I was fine as long as I was working. It was my only escape. I decided to head to my parent's house. I'd had enough inner dialogue for a lifetime, and sitting in the rental Grant and I were supposed to share as newlyweds was torture.

The weather was beautiful, so I was sure my mom would be in her rose garden. I pulled up to find her exactly where I assumed she'd be.

"Hi, Mom," I called as I spotted her in the corner, tending to her pride and joy.

"Hi, baby!" she said, throwing her gloves and trimmers onto a nearby table before hugging me. "This is a nice surprise."

"I was hoping you could use me," I said, holding up my bare, helping hands.

"Of course, your dad is out pretending to be busy. Come on." She gave me a set of gloves then we spent the afternoon caring for her garden. She was as meticulous with her yellow roses as I was with my surgery. We sat back later that day, drinking a bottle of wine and admiring our hard work.

"Thanks, Mom, I needed today."

"Is it getting any easier?"

"No, not at all. If anything, the more time passes, the more I feel like I lose him. Does that make sense?"

"Perfect sense," she said. She didn't offer any advice. She simply listened while I gave her what I could. And that's precisely what I needed, to talk about him, to remember him, and for someone to let me.

When my dad arrived, I got lost in their mindless chatter as they cooked my favorite dinner of beef stroganoff. They'd gone from a painful reminder of what could've been to a great distraction at this point. Even Dallas's newfound happiness and the recent wedding hadn't bothered me like I thought it would. Dean had fought the good fight, and I couldn't have been happier.

She got the right ending, and I couldn't be bitter because I knew she'd suffered significantly for it.

I guess seeing everyone around me happy was easier than the opposite. No one deserved the kind of battle I was dealing with. Just trying to function in the norm was still a struggle for me. I'd suffered debilitating anxiety attacks for the first few months. No matter how much I tried, Sunday nights terrorized me to no end. I was always afraid of the coming week, unsure of what might happen. I was sure that kind of thing would ruin my medical career. But when I found out I'd been accepted into McGuire's surgical residency program, I took steps to remedy my fear, pushing through to keep the one thing I had left—and it worked.

"I think we may do something other than open a general practice," I announced with a fork full of beef and noodles. This got my parents' attention.

"You and Dallas have wanted to open a practice for years," my dad said in shock.

"And we still want to do something. We've been talking about it for months, and now that Dallas is in oncology, we're thinking more along the lines of a treatment center." I looked between them as my dad sat back in his seat, chewing on the idea. "I mean, I still have years left in my surgical program, but Dallas can open while I finish." I swallowed, looking between them as they remained a captive audience. "Dad, you know I was thinking about Grant's land. Can you look into it for me and see what the asking price is? I think if we do anything, I want to do it there."

My dad looked at my mom, completely stunned.

"What?" I asked, looking at them. "I loved that land. I think it would be perfect to build on, it's right off the highway, which would mean good exposure, and Dallas agrees. The new owners haven't touched it. Grant wouldn't have wanted it to go unused."

"Rose," my mom said, taking a sip of wine as my dad excused himself from the table, "tell me what you see."

"What do you mean?" I said, thoroughly confused at my parents' sudden change in behavior. "I want to build on it, to do something with it, and possibly live there. I just keep going back to it. I know what it means to me because it was where I fell in love with Grant, but there is something else there. I can't explain it. It doesn't hurt me to be there, or at least, I don't feel like it does. It hurts me more to leave. I still want a future there. It's what made me happy."

My dad returned minutes later holding a single piece of paper that he set in front of me on the table. I looked up at him in confusion before he took his seat once again. I scanned the document, then looked at them in shock.

"We weren't sure if it was the right thing to do until you said something. We know how much you loved it there, but we just weren't sure," my dad finished, concerned by my reaction. I felt my lip tremble as I looked at my mom in disbelief. She nodded a reassuring yes, and I collapsed in a heap of tears.

"It's all yours, little woman," my dad said, wrapping his arms around me as I shook with all my weight as I cried into his chest, thanking him. "I wanted to do something, anything to ease your suffering, but I wanted to wait until you had your bearings to let you know I had obtained it. It wasn't a hard sell to the judge, and I knew how much it meant to you, Rose. I'm glad I did right by getting it."

"Dad," I said, gripping his shirt, my heart full of gratitude and my face soaked with tears. "It's the best thing you've ever given me besides my sister." As soon as I got my emotions under control, I added with a sniff, "I have to pay you back for this. You can't just give me Grant's land."

My dad smiled at me. "I can do whatever I want, Rose. It's part of the fun of being a parent. Your mom sold her motels some years back, and I've done well. We invested well. We are prepared to support you and Dallas in whatever you decide.

Think about it, and let's get to work." Overwhelmed with gratitude, I looked at them as they smiled at me. I clutched the title to me as if it would disappear. "It's done. No one will ever be able to take it from you. Do you believe me?"

I nodded in reply, still unable to put proper words together. They did an amazing thing, and I wanted them to see the happiness it brought me. I pulled in the lingering heartache and wiped away my tears with a smile.

"So, let's talk about the treatment center," my dad said excitedly. I could see the scenarios running through his mind. He was truly one of the best architects out there, and I knew the fact that this project belonged to his daughters made it an even better job for him.

"Dad, it costs millions to start what we have in mind. It's kind of unrealistic," I said, studying the paper, still in a cloud of disbelief. I hadn't lost everything.

I hadn't lost everything.

"Millions is what we have, Rose," my dad said, winking at my mom.

"What!" I asked incredulously, looking between them again. I sat stunned, waiting for the punch line.

"You've always known you and your brother and sister have a trust fund."

"Yeah, Daddy, but millions!" I looked between them, completely confused yet again. We had wanted for nothing our entire lives, but millionaires we did not live like.

"Your mom isn't a huge fan of money because she's a damn hippie. If she had it her way, we would have lived in a tent without doors or plumbing."

"Seth, you're so full of shit and way off base," my mom corrected him with a laugh. "Anyway, Rose, what your dad is trying to say is we have the money to back whatever dream you have, and what we don't have, we borrow. We want to do this. It's *our* dream to do it for you. We've been discussing it for years and praying for the day we had this conversation. You and your sister are old enough and more than responsible. Dream it up, and let's make it happen."

That night, I lay in my childhood bed dreaming big girl dreams, and for the first time since Grant died, I felt like I was taking a step in the right direction.

One and a Half Years Later

I watched Dallas and her husband, Dean, retreat happily to their car after my mom had ordered them out of the house for a night alone. Probably one of their first nights since Annabelle was born. My sister—though she whined constantly—had taken to being a mom of two in the best way, but I knew they deserved this night. I'd only managed to help with watching them a few short hours at a time since I spent most of my days in surgery. I still had a ways to go before I was certified to perform surgery independently, but in a few short months, I would be co-owner of The Grant Foster Cancer Treatment Center. I smiled as I thought of how Grant told me about his disdain and the fact that he'd never had luck with doctors, and now his name was plastered on a three-story cancer hospital. I hoped he knew and was getting a kick out of it. It was definitely a slow realization through my pain of losing it that fighting the illness alongside my sister was *exactly* where I needed to be.

It wasn't even a question as everything fell into place in

the years it took to get the place going. It was simply a matter of when.

I looked on at Dallas's babies, Grant and Annabelle, as my dad read to them about the Berenstain Bears. I couldn't believe how much those two favored their dad, Dean. And I was still oddly in awe that my sister was a mom.

Things had changed so drastically.

I stared at the babies. Both of them had brilliant blue eyes and black hair. The only way I could tell they belonged to my sister was by their personalities. And Lord have mercy on us all for that. I chuckled as Grant squirmed loose of my dad and came running towards me. His grin was devilish, and his dimples showed as he ran into my arms, tackling me. It hadn't taken me long to fall in love with him. I would say as long as it did his predecessor of the same name. It was love at first sight. The minute Grant Jeffrey Martin was born, I had a new purpose. Although being an aunt wasn't what most would call a life goal, it meant more to me than anything.

"Aunt Wose, you and me sleep in de fort tonight?" Grant asked, his chubby cheeks and sweet smell my undoing.

"Of course," I said, picking him up and holding him close.

"Aunt Wose, I don't want Annabelle da come," he said directly into my ear, making me giggle at the tickle.

"Okay, buddy, I'll make sure Grandpa keeps her away."

"Let's go fast!" He urged me up the stairs so Annabelle couldn't follow. I obliged, lifting him quickly up the stairs as his chubby hand nestled in my hair at the back of my neck—a habit he'd formed when he was just months old. It warmed me to no end.

We sat up for hours, building our fort and playing underneath it. He told me about his day and an incident with yogurt while I taught him the names of the bones in his arms and hand. Grant finally drifted to sleep, and my mom peeked in and whispered goodnight. I lay next to him, watching his chest rise and fall.

I'd been beyond touched when my sister informed me she was naming her firstborn Grant. And although it stung at times, I couldn't see him with any other name. He didn't look a thing like the man I'd lost, but his beating heart reminded me of him daily. The baby had taken my entire heart over in a matter of minutes and refused to let go. And as I held him, I remembered thinking that was the kind of love I'd thought I'd lost forever. Loving my nephew the way I did reminded me that I was still capable, and though I'd suffered the worst loss imaginable, it let me know I was still there.

Watching the sweet saccharin drip from his mouth, I smiled. My Grant wouldn't have wanted me to give up. I knew deep down that I would eventually have to try again. My thoughts drifted to the man I'd just spent the night with. He was part of the reason I'd cowered to my parents. I didn't know what to think about what we'd done. He'd been the first since I'd lost Grant.

With Jack, I'd managed to capture a small piece of me that I hadn't realized still existed. The passion in which he'd taken me felt beyond good, yet the guilt I felt after leaving his bed was enough to level me. I didn't want to be reminded how much further my life with Grant had drifted away with that one act.

Grant was no longer the last man that had touched me.

I closed my eyes, stifling a sob. That alone might be too much to bear. I drifted to sleep thinking of the first time Grant had ever kissed me. His strong arms braced on either side of his kneeling stance as he leaned in and pressed his soft full lips to mine. I dreamed of his tender kiss and the words that echoed throughout my body and through my thoughts daily on repeat, letting me know that what I had and lost was truly exceptional and could never be replaced.

"Did you feel that?"

I opened my eyes, hearing his voice with clarity, noting it had only been a short hour since I closed them. I pulled the covers over Grant and turned on my side to gaze out the bedroom window. I did what I always do and remembered Grant's and my time from beginning to end. Maybe it was a sadistic ritual, but I'd made him a promise, and it was one I intended to keep.

His life was not in vain. He would not be forgotten. As sad as the ritual might've been, I had no intention of letting go of it. It was for me and in honor of the man that would never let me forget that at one time, I was one romantic madly in love with another.

I replayed our short time together, right down to the very last time he spoke to me.

"One week, Mr. Foster. Are you sure you don't want to change your mind?"

"One week and forever, baby. I promise."

He promised.

No, no one will want to hear our story anymore because it doesn't have the ending that they want, but for Grant, I will always tell it.

The Mind Spotify playlist
https://spotify.link/gxyKEcgPaDb

about the
author

USA Today bestselling author and Texas native, Kate Stewart, lives in North Carolina with her husband, Nick. Nestled within the Blue Ridge Mountains, Kate pens messy, sexy, angst-filled contemporary romance, as well as romantic comedy and erotic suspense.

Kate's title, *Drive*, was named one of the best romances of 2017 by The New York Daily News and Huffington Post. *Drive* was also a finalist in the Goodreads Choice awards for best contemporary romance of 2017. The Ravenhood Trilogy, consisting of *Flock, Exodus*, and *The Finish Line*, has become an international bestseller and reader favorite. Her holiday release, *The Plight Before Christmas*, ranked #6 on Amazon's Top 100. Kate's works have been featured in *USA TODAY, BuzzFeed, The New York Daily News, Huffington Post* and translated into a dozen languages.

Kate is a lover of all things '80s and '90s, especially John Hughes films and rap. She dabbles a little in photography, can knit a simple stitch scarf for necessity, and on occasion, does very well at whiskey.

Other titles available now by Kate

Romantic Suspense

The Ravenhood Series
Flock
Exodus
The Finish Line

The Ravenhood Legacy
One Last Rainy Day: The Legacy of a Prince

Lust & Lies Series
Sexual Awakenings
Excess
Predator and Prey

Contemporary Romance

In Reading Order

Room 212
Never Me (Companion to Room 212 and The Reluctant Romantic Series)
The Reluctant Romantics Series
The Fall
The Mind
The Heart
The Reluctant Romantics Box Set: The Fall, The Heart, The Mind
Loving the White Liar

The Bittersweet Symphony
Drive
Reverse
Bittersweet Melody

The Real
Someone Else's Ocean
Heartbreak Warfare
Method

Romantic Dramedy

Balls in Play Series
Anything but Minor
Major Love
Sweeping the Series Novella

The Underdogs Series
The Guy on the Right
The Guy on the Left
The Guy in the Middle

The Plight Before Christmas

Let's stay in touch!

Join my reader group - Kate Stewart's Recovery Room

Order Merch and Signed Copies - www.katestewartwrites.com

Facebook
www.facebook.com/authorkatestewart

Newsletter
www.katestewartwrites.com/contact-me.html

Twitter
twitter.com/authorklstewart

Instagram
www.instagram.com/authorkatestewart/?hl=en

Spotify
open.spotify.com/user/authorkatestewart